THE STEWARDESS'S DIARY - PART NINE

JAPAN

S.M. PRATT

The Stewardess's Diary - Part Nine: Japan
Copyright © 2017 by S.M. Pratt

Last updated January 25th, 2020
Editing by Samantha Marie

ISBN: 978-1-988639-02-4 (e-book)

ISBN: 978-1-988639-28-4 (paperback)

I'M CHARLIE, a veteran pilot for a major international airline that shall remain nameless for reasons you'll soon come to understand.

A year ago, while waiting for my flight to London in the airline's lounge at one of America's largest hubs, I discovered a special and highly personal journal among my belongings. How it happened, I'll never know, but the beautiful brown leather notebook nonetheless appeared in my briefcase at some point between the time I left my New York penthouse apartment and arrived at the airport lounge.

Perhaps it was a mix-up at security, or some devious stewardess with sly hand skills, but I've since become obsessed with the person who wrote that diary, her stories, and—to be blunt—her unconventional sex life.

My best friend—let's call him Bob—is one of my regular co-pilots. Bob advised me to forget about the journal and ignore my hunch to track down its rightful owner. After my initial reading of her hand-written accounts, the part of me who's loyal to the airline and wants the best for our passengers certainly needed to find that stewardess and expel her from our company—or whatever airline she's with. This woman is surely a threat to any crew with her irreverent disregard for our uniforms, her sexual behavior with passengers and airline employees, and the way she ignores regulations. She should clearly be punished for her conduct...

But after reading and re-reading each one of her journal entries, another, more animal part of me has grown fond of her complete lack of boundaries, her willingness to experiment, and her ravenous sexual appetite.

I've had my fair share of illicit affairs with female flight attendants and co-pilots, but none of them were interesting enough to be granted a second fuck by yours truly, let alone be courted or considered for a long-term relationship. But the woman who's filled so many pages with delicate calligraphy and salacious words deserves my full attention. She's certainly maintained it well past the time I closed the cover of her journal—again and again.

Imagining how her naiveté was gradually—and most willingly—robbed from her was simply... enthralling. She's been haunting my wet dreams.

Now, every time I see an unknown stewardess, I wonder if *she*'s the one.

After many conversations with Bob over the past months during our overseas flights, I've come to share some of her journal entries with him. He agrees that I need to locate her. If not for the airline's sake or to satisfy my personal curiosity, then for the mere reason that I could stop obsessing about her and resume paying attention to my actual job: piloting giant aircrafts and safely getting passengers from point A to point B.

The following short stories record my obsession toward her. There are ten in total. Each installment contains my mystery stewardess's original journal entries for a specific location, followed by my own experiences in trying to track her down. You'll discover what (and whom) I did in an effort to identify and locate my stewardess based on the clues she's left in her diary. You can read the episodes in any order, but they'll probably make more sense if you start from the beginning and follow along as I attempt to find her.

And, just to be clear, these stories should *not* land in the hands of any prude or underage person. Some are just romantic, sensual, or highly erotic, while others are immoral, perverse, and possibly even illegal in some parts of the world.

Ah, the things I'll do to this mystery stewardess when I finally encounter her in the flesh!

I'm hard just thinking about it...

Yours truly,

Capt. Charlie
Undisclosed Airline

PART ONE

THE STEWARDESS'S ENTRIES

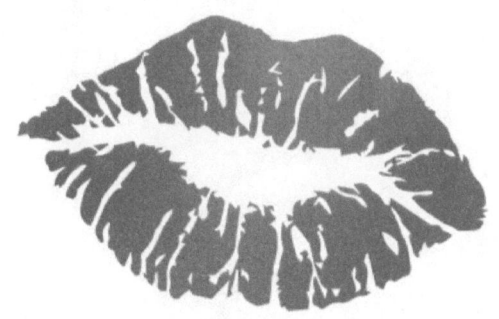

ALEX HANDED me a red silky envelope covered with vertical streams of Japanese characters. "Then there's this event," she said.

I accepted the document and let my fingers graze the beautiful calligraphy. "What is it?"

"It's a private function hosted by Mr. Suzuki. That man's wealthier than anyone I know. No clue what it will be about this year, but it's sure to be a blast. Our kind of fun, if you know what I mean... He invites lots of beautiful people."

"Certainly beats staying in my hotel room. What should I wear?"

Alex raised her shoulders. "I don't know, but you can't go wrong with a black evening gown."

"And how will I get there?"

"The address is inside. Just show the card to your hotel concierge or taxi driver."

I turned the envelope over and noticed the opening was on one of the small ends. I tapped it against my hand and a thick card slid out, which was also covered in characters I couldn't read or understand.

"And when is it exactly?"

"Ah! *That* I did find out. Those characters are the date and time," she said, pointing at the second line from the right. "The evening on the day you land. That should give you enough time for a solid afternoon nap, then the event starts at 9 o'clock. I guess you'll have to figure out the address first so you can plan ahead in terms of travel time from your hotel."

"Taking over your flights certainly comes with added benefits," I said. "Thanks, and good luck with your mom."

"I'm just glad you were qualified for that aircraft so I could hand you my ticket. Mr. Suzuki doesn't host events that everyone enjoys, but I know I will absolutely love it, whatever it ends up being. You'll have to tell me all about it when I see you next."

"I will."

"Okay, I gotta go now, so I can get there before her surgery."

I gave her a big hug then watched her disappear toward her departure gate.

WITH THE UPCOMING mysterious event on my mind, the past days had flown by. I really had no idea what Alex meant other than there could be some opportunities to have sex with beautiful people. Or perhaps she meant some 4:20 activities, but the latter seemed unlikely.

But now that I was in Tokyo, refreshed by my afternoon nap, I was once again day-dreaming about what would be happening in a couple of hours from now. Would it be some sort of 70s-inspired event where men put their keychains in a bowl and women randomly picked one and went home with its owner?

That could be fun.

Or maybe it would be something classier that

would still involve nudity. Like a naked musical. *That's not very Japanese now, is it?*

The alarm clock by my bed indicated it was time to go.

I double-checked my makeup and outfit in the mirror. My hairdo was still looking good, with just the right number of strands cascading out of my loose chignon. I smoothed out my long black dress and got rid of a few pieces of loose threads that had somehow clung to its silky fabric.

My necklace!

I walked to my carry-on and dug it out. I'd brought a simple silver circle that hung on a delicate chain. It wasn't worth much, but its simplicity turned it into the perfect accessory in a pinch.

My black clutch under my arm, I headed out of my room and down to the reception to get myself a cab.

THE TAXI SLOWED DOWN as it approached a large industrial building. Had it not been for a few people spilling out of the vehicles in front of me, I'd have been worried my driver was going to murder me in an abandoned factory.

But a man in a kimono walked up to the cab as we came to a halt in front of the entrance. As he opened my door, I handed money to the driver, then stepped out of the cab.

"*Konbanwa*," said the man in the kimono as he helped me out of the vehicle.

"Good evening," I said, feeling awful for not even having bothered to learn a few Japanese phrases before coming here. But my guilt morphed into excitement as quickly as it had come.

The man pointed toward the entrance, and I joined the guests waiting to enter the building.

A short woman—also wearing a kimono—stood by the door. She first said something in Japanese, then, since I didn't understand, she asked in English: "Can I see your invitation please?"

"Here it is," I said, handing her my envelope.

"Follow the other women in front of you, to your right."

As Alex had predicted, I was surrounded by beautiful people in assorted skin tones. I saw a tall, handsome blond guy—my type down to a T— being ushered to a different part of the building toward the left.

Maybe I'll see him again later.

The women in front of me had already moved ahead, so I hurried my pace—as fast as my high heels let me—and I caught up to them as they entered a very large room. About thirty kimono-wearing staff were lined up along the front wall. In the middle of the room, chairs were paired with their own small tables, as though I'd walked into a speed-dating event.

Is this it? A speed-dating evening?

I joined the rest of the guests in the center of the room. Everyone kept quiet. I smiled at those who made eye contact with me. The silence made me feel a little ill-at-ease, adding to my existing discomfort stemming from not knowing what was going to happen this evening. I was about to talk to a black woman standing near me when one of the kimonoed staff spoke up in the microphone.

After saying something in Japanese, he added English instructions: "Please pick your assistant. He or she will help you all evening with the games." His hand pointed toward the line-up of men and women in matching outfits behind him.

Games?

Not knowing what I'd need assisting with, I picked a tall young man with a faint smile on his face. His silky black hair was parted to the side, and his long bangs cascaded in a loose loop down his ivory forehead before being tucked behind his left ear. Although long at the top, the rest of his hair was cut short at the nape. He looked like he was twenty at most.

"My name is Junichi," he said, bowing in front of me.

I bowed as well, unsure what proper Japanese etiquette called for here.

His smile got wider, and he directed me toward a set of chairs in the center of the room. "We will go through the agreement for the games. It's written in Japanese, so I will translate it for you."

"Okay," I said as he placed a questionnaire in front of me, along with a pen.

"Write your first name here and your family name here." He pointed toward specific fields on the form.

I wrote them in.

"Date of birth: year, month, day."

After I filled out the numbers he needed, he translated a series of yes/no questions having to do with my health: "Was I menstruating right now? Was I allergic to latex? Did I have sexually transmitted diseases?" The list was much longer, but those are the ones I recall.

The sound of chairs backing up on the concrete floor made me turn around during those questions. The black woman I'd nearly approached earlier had gotten up and was walking out the door. So was a tall blonde woman.

Junichi spoke up, "We have more questions to answer. If you feel uncomfortable, then you are free to leave."

My inner competitive self wanted to know if I'd stomach whatever these women were opposed to. So I let Junichi translate the next batch of questions: "Was I comfortable in front of a camera? Was I opposed to pre-marital sex? Was I open to intercourse with men? Was I comfortable with nudity? Was I okay with anal sex? Would I shave hair from certain body parts?"

"As long as you're not asking me to shave my head!" I said.

He smiled. "No, no."

"Then fine."

The first side of the questionnaire now completed, he flipped to another page. While he was fumbling with the document, I glanced around the room once more. The initial group of women had dwindled down by about a third.

On the new page sitting in front of me, a long paragraph appeared, followed by ¥10000000 and a line to sign on.

"What does this say?" I asked Junichi.

"This is the total prize amount if you win. There will also be smaller prizes for all participants. You need to sign on the dotted line."

"There's gotta be more than what you just told me," I said, worried I was signing my life away. "The paragraph almost covers the entire page."

He brought the document closer to him and translated it as he read it:

"It says that you agree to participate in the recording of a private video, along with other men and women. You also agree to partake in all of the events of this game, which may include physical contact or other activities of a sexual nature, including objectification of the body."

For the chance of winning ten million yen? What is that? Around $80,000?

"So, it will not be a public video?" I asked.

"No, it's for Mr. Suzuki and his wife. But there's a crew filming the games, so they'll see you and the other contestants, but they're not allowed to record using their own equipment.

Only one life to live! Might as well make it count. And maybe the hot blond guy will be paired with me...

I signed on the dotted line.

"Perfect," he said as he took the signed contract and pen from my hands. He stood up. "Now we'll get you prepared. Please follow me to the next room."

I got up and joined him in the preparation area, which reminded me of a very large gym locker room, complete with lockers, showers, toilets... and a whole crew of kimono-wearing Japanese men and women.

He instructed me to use the washroom and empty anything I may have in my body as this was going to be my last opportunity, then to hop in the shower.

9:15 P.M.

EVEN THOUGH I'D showered just hours earlier, I obeyed.

I disrobed and placed my belongings in a locker, then headed into the shower, along with about a dozen other women. Some tall, some short, some athletic, some chubby, some skinny, but all were beautiful in their own way. While walking butt-naked to the shower hadn't bothered me, I expected the open communal shower with its multiple shower heads to do the trick, but no.

My, my. How I've grown.

I no longer worried about women judging me. I was finally comfortable in my own skin. I wasn't even paying attention to those around me... That was until a woman with elaborate puffed-up hair tried to leave the shower with her 'do still dry.

A uniformed man was shaking his head at her, pointing her back toward the shower.

She put up a fuss. At least that's what I understood of her flailing arms and loud outburst in a language I didn't recognize. *Russian?*

For a few seconds, they stood there, as though dueling with their minds: the woman with her hands on her hips, the man with his arms crossed on his chest. Then, the woman's assistant, a petite Japanese woman, brought the upset contestant a large towel and escorted her away from the shower area.

Seconds later, our assistants came up to the shower entrance and yelled to us over the running water. "You must wash your hair or else you'll be expelled from the game," said Junichi.

I nodded.

The games had me too intrigued to worry about my hairdo.

After shampooing and conditioning my hair with the products provided to us, I was as clean as I could ever be. At least that was true for my body; my mind was a different story. I kept thinking about that blond man and what I'd like to do to him or have him do to me.

I walked out of the tiled area, and Junichi handed me a towel.

Once I dried myself off, I wrapped the oversized piece of plush material around me and followed Junichi to an area with more uniformed women. A few massage tables and elevated pedicure chairs had been installed here.

One of the women reached toward me and unwrapped my towel before proceeding to scrutinize my body. She asked me to sit on the massage table (Junichi translated her requests as she talked), then she inspected my armpits and my pussy. I'd gotten my hair waxed a couple of days prior, but I'd requested to keep my narrow landing strip. The woman obviously had something against it since she grabbed a manual razor and a can of shaving cream then proceeded to remove what little hair remained to differentiate my pussy from that of a pre-teen girl.

"Lean back on the table," Junichi translated after the woman spoke.

I obeyed, and the woman parted my legs, then my butt cheeks, inspecting me like cattle. I knew there was no other hair to remove. Come to think of it, I was a bit surprised that the woman had used a razor, but if they were going to be filming us, it probably made more sense than waxing, which could have left behind unsightly red bumps.

She then looked at my fingers and toes, inspecting each of my digits for the status of my red gel manicure.

She nodded, said something to Junichi, and then he translated her next request: "Please sit on the chair. She will comb your hair and tie it in a ponytail."

I followed their instructions. Then, a touch of makeup later, I was free to leave but not with just one ponytail. My hair had been parted right in the middle, and the woman had tied two ponytails with red ribbons, one on each side of my head.

Last time my hair had been done up like this was more than 25 or 30 years ago?

"We have about thirty minutes before the first game. Would you like a massage to relax?" asked Junichi.

Who turns down a free massage offer? "Of course! I'd love a massage," I said.

I followed Junichi to another area, this one populated with several tables and a handful of naked women receiving massages from their male or female assistants. Music played softly in the background, something similar in tone to Barry White, but in Japanese.

I lay down on my stomach, and Junichi began spreading a sweet-smelling lotion on my back, then my arms and legs. His fingers got a hold of one of my feet, and he began kneading my skin. Both my feet were worked on, then calves, then thighs. His slow, magical touch had me so relaxed.

Once he finished with my legs, he moved on to my shoulders and worked out the knots. His digits squeezed away the stress that had accumulated, allowing my mind to wander while my eyes were closed. I imagined the handsome blond man working on my back instead of Junichi. Each stroke and caress I received suddenly triggered a different reaction in my body. Something more instinctual, more intense, more primal.

By the time Junichi reached my lower back, I was craving hands on my ass and between my legs. Unfortunately, my wish wasn't fulfilled. Instead, he moved his attention to my fingers and arms, offering a soothing massage nonetheless.

But my mind had already been turned on; my inner fantasy world had already ignited desires that I hoped these mysterious games would fulfill.

A LOUD ALARM rang in the room, bringing my delightful massage and fantasies to a screeching halt before letting them crash into a figurative concrete wall.

"Time to go. The games will begin," Junichi said.

I got up and followed him. The rest of the women in the group were doing the same. With all the female contestants naked, it was easy to differentiate us from the assistants.

As we walked through various doors, then along a windy path backstage, Junichi told me more about the games. "This is how it works: We prepare for one game, then we record it live once. There's only one chance for each game, no second takes. Then, the recording stops, and we prepare for the second game. When we're ready, we record it live. We repeat the process for each game. Understood?"

I nodded. "Do they explain the rules in English?"

"I'll translate them for you," he said.

I overheard the short brunette in front of me ask a question to her assistant in an Australian accent: "How many games are there?"

"It depends on the points earned by each participant, but up to ten games," her assistant replied.

I turned to Junichi. "So, we'll be here for what... two hours?" I asked.

"No, more like all night."

11:00 P.M.

JUNICHI TOOK me to the first game room. It looked pretty bare to me, except for a series of tall vertical boxes lined up against the longest wall, each with a small container in front of it. The room had no ceiling. Instead, bright lights, cameras, microphone booms, and other devices chaotically hung above us.

A loud voice boomed from an overhead speaker, first in Japanese, then in English: "Ladies, please pick a pod."

Like the other women around me, I headed toward the back wall and selected one of the tall vertical boxes.

Junichi, who had quietly followed me to the pod, walked past me. "Please step over the ledge and get in, with your back against the fabric, facing me."

The more I looked at it, the more I saw a vertical coffin, but I obeyed, stepping over the foot-high divide, and then turning around to rest my back against the soft, black, velvety fabric behind me. When I pushed my body against it, its plushness hugged me like a thick, comfortable memory-foam mattress.

Junichi opened the square box in front of the pod, which revealed a bunch of dark gray planks. He carried then slid these planks into small grooves above my pod's threshold. Each plank slowly but surely confined me into a closed box. Junichi stopped when he reached my belly button.

Just when I thought I'd been boxed in enough, I watched him head toward the box and return with one more plank, this one a little less thick than the others he'd brought. The plank also had two holes on one side.

"Watch your head, I need to bring this one in," he said.

I backed up some more into the soft mattress behind me.

He moved his hands into my pod and reached toward the top. Instead of sliding this plank into place, he hung it from two tiny hooks in front of me, way above my head. I hadn't noticed those before. The thin plank now in place, less light was coming into my pod, but I could still see three hooks at the base of the new plank, which ended just above my head. Then, as I pondered about the purpose of these hooks (and realized I was thankfully just short of touching them should I move forward), I watched him walk toward the box again. He came back with a piece of rolled fabric.

"I need to attach this to the piece above. Please close your eyes," he said.

I did while also pushing my head back as far as I could. I heard fumbling noises for a few seconds, then nothing.

"You can open your eyes again," he said.

I did and saw that a black meshing had been rolled down to around my chin, blocking more light from coming into the box, but I could still see movement in front of me.

"Step forward, please. Put your feet in the recess in front of you and bring your stomach so it's flat against the planks," Junichi said.

By stepping closer to the fabric, my eyesight improved. In fact, I could even recognize Junichi's face while he stood right in front of me. He was looking at me, focusing on my stomach and breasts, a slight frown on his face. I assumed he must have measured something with his hand as I watched him keep a specific distance between his fingers while he compared planks to his held-out hand.

He came back with another plank a few seconds later. It was about as wide as what he'd just measured.

"Please back up again."

I did.

He slid that latest plank down the front, then asked me to step forward again, his hands up in the air. "I'll touch your breasts and bring them up so they don't get squished," he said. He gently got a hold of my breasts and rested them above the plank. "Stay there, I'll move the back of the pod forward. Please tell me to stop when you feel the mattress behind you. Don't worry. It won't hurt, and I'll be right back."

I swallowed hard, then nodded.

He disappeared out of sight, walking between my pod and the next. Then, as promised, I started feeling the space shrink behind me. The soft velvet touched my ass.

"Stop," I said.

He came around to the front and looked at me.

"I need to close the space a lot more for the game to work."

I didn't like the idea, but couldn't do much about it either.

Junichi once again disappeared out of my sight, and soon enough the mattress behind me started moving forward.

"Stop!" I yelped when the planks in front of me squished my stomach.

He came back. "Push yourself back as far as you can," he said.

"I *am* as far back as I can! My stomach is against the planks. I can't move!" My heart pounded in my chest, but me trying to breathe deeper just increased my level of pain and discomfort.

"I'll move it back a little bit."

A few seconds later, after he did, I sighed in relief.

"Are you more comfortable now?" he asked when he reappeared in front of me.

"Better," I said. "Am I going to stay in this coffin for a long time?"

"No, this game will be fast. But I have one more plank to add. I need to cover the space above your breasts all the way to your nose."

"Whoa..."

"Don't worry, you'll still be able to breathe and see what's going on around you. You won't be in any danger during the game, I promise."

"Okay."

Obviously, since all the pods were one next to the other, I couldn't see the other women from my vantage point, but I could only assume they were all being prepared the same way I was. I exhaled loudly as I watched my assistant come back with one large plastic plank with U-shaped cords on two sides opposite each other. He reached around one side of my pod, then the other, which seemed to secure that last plank in place.

I'm a freaking coffin with boobs! What kind of game is this going to be?

I saw Junichi and other assistants walking out of the room holding the boxes with whatever had been left in them, then they each reappeared with rolling trays covered with goodies I couldn't quite identify from where I stood.

After rolling his tray in the center of the room, in front of my pod, Junichi headed toward me.

"The preparations are almost over. The first game will start soon. I'll be back to help you out as soon as it's over."

"Okay. Do I need to do anything during the game?"

"No, you just stand there in silence. Easy, right?"

"I guess," was all I could say, but butterflies tried to flicker in my constricted stomach.

With that, he disappeared from view again. More assistants rolled their trays in the middle of the room, and then nothing happened for a couple of minutes.

The lights suddenly got brighter and loud music from old-school porn movies started playing. It was so tacky I expected a man's voice to say, "I'm here to clean your pool."

But before I could reminisce any more about the first porn movie I'd ever seen, a loud Japanese voice with the excitement of a late-night infomercial salesman announced something. Unfortunately for me, no translation was provided.

I had absolutely no idea what was to come. A loud buzzer rang for three seconds, then a group of men ran into the room.

1, 2, 3... I counted twenty of them. All naked, with skin shades from the darkest of blacks to the whitest of whites I'd ever seen. They took their positions, lining themselves up across the room in front of the pods, in pairs.

In front of me, next to a very well endowed black man, a tall and muscular red-headed man and a slender Asian man stood, their dicks relaxed. I squinted and was surprised to see that the red-headed man packed smaller equipment than the Asian man. *So much for stereotypes, but limp dicks sometimes prove surprising. Hmm... I've never been with an Asian man before. Why is that?*

But before I could even venture a guess to my own meanderings, a loud horn sounded and the men started racing toward our row of pods. The red-headed man and the Asian man approached me nearly at the same speed.

A few seconds later, my breasts were slapped, one after the other. Then the men turned around and raced back to their starting line.

My flesh stung, and the edge of the upper plank dug in the underside of my flesh as my breasts bounced back to their previous position.

What the fuck? Is this a breast-slapping game?

I kept my eyes on both men: they had run back to the start line, then turned around and sprinted back toward me again.

Oh no... Not again. The closer they got, the more I tensed in anticipation. I closed my eyes, ready to scream if they did it again.

But before I could burst out in anger, my girls each received a kiss on the nipple, followed by a gentle squeeze.

I reopened my eyes. The men were once again sprinting away from me, but this time they stopped by the tray in the middle of the room. They came back with a small bowl and something else I couldn't quite recognize.

When they reached me again, something warm got painted on my breasts. Chocolate aroma drifted up to my nose. The red-headed man finished my right breast first. By the time the Asian man had finished my other breast, the first man had left and reappeared with a can of whipped cream in front of me. I heard the pressurized air escape and felt a cool circle being drawn around my right breast, then a tiny circle around my nipple. As both men returned to their goody tray, my Asian boob decoration lagging by a step, I noticed that they both looked up toward the center of the room, but high above.

Is there a display with instructions on what to do next?

They returned to me again, and I was unsure of what they were going to do this time. Their facial expressions were focused on the task at hand. Pearls of sweat beaded on the red-headed man's freckled forehead. The Asian man was much shorter and didn't show any signs of sweat or stress.

I, like the red-headed man, was starting to perspire inside my pod. I didn't particularly like being in my coffin-like box, but at least my breasts weren't being slapped again.

A gong sounded.

Both men bent down out of my field of vision before their wet mouth and tongue began licking and sucking on my exposed skin. Although rushed, their actions were delightful. My left breast suddenly stopped receiving its treatment; I watched the Asian man run back toward the start line. When he turned around to sprint back toward me, I saw his chocolate-, whipping-cream-, and rainbow-sprinkled cheeks.

His final move?

A twist of my nipple, which I didn't expect, nor like. He then lifted both of his hands up in the air. My other nipple got twisted and the two men double high-fived each other.

What did I get myself into?

12:00 A.M.

AFTER WE ALL got a chance to rinse off, then get ourselves dry, we were taken to a large rectangular room with an assortment of strange, squiggly upside-down Y-shaped boxes about four feet tall. The lower part, which inclined toward the floor, was split into two, while the upper part was more upright. Behind the latter was a door.

"Pick a pod. Open the door and sit on the stool," Junichi whispered in my ear. "More instructions will be provided shortly."

I proceeded as directed and so did the other women around me. I picked a pod near the back corner, but before I reached for the small silver door knob, I couldn't resist the urge to touch the odd-looking fabric that covered the enclosure. It was soft and bouncy, reminding me of those stress-relief rubber balls I once used.

I opened my door. The pod contained a stool with a very low back, so I stepped in, sat on the seat, but there was no room for my legs in front of me. The pod's odd Y-shape forced me to spread my legs so they could fit in the two slots that dangled down. From my seated position, I could see through a meshed screen I hadn't noticed before.

A few straggling women each entered their own pod, then a Japanese voice boomed over the speaker.

Between my legs, about six inches in front of me, an oval hole, about four inches wide and six inches high, was clearly visible.

Junichi came up behind me while the pod door was still open. "Are your legs in place?" he asked.

"I think so?"

"Looks like it," he said while poking his head above my shoulder. "Just relax. I'll lower your seat and move you forward."

He adjusted my position, then came around the front. He pressed a button, and I felt myself drop. Green light shone between my legs when the small panel lifted.

"Move forward on your seat," he ordered.

I scooched up by about an inch, blocking most of the green luminescence.

"Perfect," he said. "I'll bring you back up. Don't move."

A loud click sounded, and I was lifted up.

A few seconds later, Junichi was once again standing behind me. "You may want to warm yourself up so the game is more enjoyable." He closed the door behind me, leaving me wondering what was to come.

Soon enough, the porn soundtrack from the earlier game resumed, along with loud grunts of people fucking and coming. From the meshed window in front of me, I noticed the previously white walls of the room had turned into screens where a porn movie was being projected.

Scratch that: several porn movies.

There was one very talented young blonde handling five men at once: one fucking her in the front, one in her ass, one in her mouth, and one in each of her hands. Then to my left, there was a lone brunette playing in the shower with a purple dildo. In front of me, a tiny Asian woman was being taken in the ass by a large black man. Further to the right, a single man appeared, hot as hell. Like one of those underwear models, except he didn't have any underwear on. Just his chiseled abs, his strong, lean muscles, and his hard cock in hand. He was wanking off, staring right at the camera. Right at me, or so it seemed. I started warming myself up while focusing on him. Among the mishmash of soundtracks, I found his and tried to focus on his grunts as I touched myself, matching the speed of my finger to the cadence of his fist as it went up and down his beautiful shaft.

Then I closed my eyes and imagined his hands on my breasts and stomach as I grazed my own skin in the privacy of my pod. I took away his pretty face and replaced it with that of the handsome blond man I'd seen earlier today. I kept the rest of the porn star's body though. *Hot Blondie.* By now, my opening was slick with excitement, I'd added a second digit and could hear my own moisture echo softly in my enclosure as I fingered myself faster and faster.

Then, a horn sounded, taking me away from Fantasyland, yet again.

I reopened my eyes and took my hand away from my pussy. The same group of naked men was now coming into the room, each running toward our enclosures. I spotted red-headed man for a second, but he disappeared behind another pod. I couldn't see my handsome blond man among the crowd in my vision field. But a brown-haired man was coming my way. His chest hair was similar to what most 80s rock-band singers would have proudly shown off during live shows back in the days.

Funny how they didn't feel the need to shave chest hair...

A second later, my seat got lowered and the same green light reappeared. A cool breeze greeted my warm pussy, then pressure was applied to the rubbery surface that surrounded my exposed lips.

With a hesitant poke, the hairy man's dick parted my insides. I let out a quiet moan, glad to have warmed myself up ahead of time. Not that he was that big, but my self-entertainment had been the only foreplay here.

Then came a second thrust, this one much more powerful and confident. Then another and another. Being fucked without feeling the warmth of another person's body was odd, but I closed my eyes and played with my clit instead, pretending everything was normal, getting more and more aroused, pretending he was Blondie.

But it stopped suddenly. I opened my eyes and the hairy man was running away, his white butt and hairless back racing out of sight, leaving my pussy hanging high and wet.

Other men were doing the same. Then, a mere minute later, the walls returned to white, the music ended, and my assistant was once again talking to me behind the pod.

"This game is over. I'll raise your seat, then open your door and help you get out."

I wiped my pussy, but I didn't know what to do with my hand.

I stepped out of my pod and accepted the bathrobe Junichi handed me. I looked around at the other women and their confused faces. I must admit that my own expression was probably similar to theirs. An Indian woman started giggling nervously, then so did the Australian woman I'd heard before. She was standing a few feet away. Then the whole room joined her, myself included.

I'd seen Japanese game shows on TV before, but I couldn't say that I'd seen any of the adult-themed variety. I'd never watched them to the end because I found them so freaking confusing, so I had no idea what was in store for me and the rest of the contestants.

I could only assume I'd get my fair share of fucking tonight, and from random strangers at that.

The likelihood of anyone I knew ever watching this game show was nonexistent, but I still wondered what I'd gotten myself into.

OUR GROUP WAS ESCORTED out of the room and taken to a different area.

Calling it a *room* would have been pushing it. It was more like that secret passageway in the *maison close* I recently saw in Paris, but much wider. We were standing behind the unfinished backside of a set, probably not where the contestants would be competing.

We followed the lead assistant in a tour of sorts, walking as a group. But each time our guide came across an available slot, one woman stayed behind with her assistant while the rest of us kept going. I had no idea what the slots looked like on the other side of the set, but from where I stood, they were just body-sized recesses where we had to stand, but the wall seemed to be partly open in two spots in front of those recesses: one about a third of the way, and the other two-thirds of the height.

The third recess surprised me. Instead of being vertical like the others, it was horizontal, just off of the floor.

Then we passed another horizontal slot that required climbing up a short ladder. The black woman selected it and proceeded to go up, followed by her assistant.

We made our way around the bend, and our group slowly shrank in size as more and more contestants selected their own recess as we spotted them. We turned another corner after losing yet a few more women to more vertical and horizontal slots. I had no real incentive to rush, so I was part of the last two women who had yet to select a recess by the time we had walked around the full perimeter of the room.

Back at our starting point, the two of us were instructed to go up a ladder to the top of the room.

Once up there, I was surprised by the geometry of the ceiling. It wasn't flat as I'd expected it to be. It was more like a series of large blocks randomly piled next to each other. In fact, it made me think about what the top layer of a Tetris board would look like as a 3D game.

But Junichi took me out of my childhood memories and told me to pick a position.

I selected the next one I saw, something perpendicular to a slot the other woman had already taken.

"Rest with your face down."

I did, my arms relaxed by my side. Gravity did its thing and pulled my breasts down, away from my body. And the cooler air in the room below made me realize I had started sweating underneath the fold of my breasts. The other open area was lined up with my belly button. Other than that, it didn't feel too weird. Thankfully, the surface was well padded and very sturdy, but the two spaces where planks were missing didn't quite line up with my body.

"Lift your hips," Junichi asked of me.

I pressed my toes into the surface below me and straightened my legs, raising my entire lower body off from the padded surface. I turned to look at him.

He slid one of the padded planks up toward the hole where my breasts hung, then another.

"Lower your body again."

He was looking at my hips and the planks.

"You're aligned now. Perfect."

He walked up closer to my face. "Here's a

pillow for your head, and an applicator. Insert it like you would a tampon."

"What?" I asked.

"It's not a real tampon; it's for the next game. And don't worry, it's made of clean material. It won't stay inside you for very long."

I rolled over to my side, then to my back. I sat up to perform the task he'd requested of me. While I'd grown accustomed to walking around naked for these games, I couldn't say the same about inserting a tampon in me. Real or not. It somehow felt more... personal.

As though he understood my inner conundrum, a second later, he turned around.

I parted my legs, removed the plastic cover, then brought the tip of the applicator to my pussy before pushing it in. It slid in like a normal tampon. The device in place with its super long string hanging out, I put the applicator back in the plastic cover.

"I'm done," I said, and Junichi turned around.

He took the wrapper I was holding. "Lay down in position again. Make yourself comfortable."

I obeyed, then turned my head to look at him. "Do I have to do anything?" I asked.

"No. Just stay there. Don't move and don't speak. When the game is over, you'll hear it. Then you can come back down and I'll meet you by the ladder."

He left me alone with my thoughts.

Soon porn music started playing again.

What is the fucking goal of this game? Objectification of women? Is it a cultural thing? First tit-slapping, then faceless pussy fucking—without a happy ending might I add—and now this weird boob and tampon game?

And how the fuck am I supposed to win this game or increase the money I'll make if I don't even get to do anything? I'm all for new experiences, but isn't this a bit too... passive?

A loud horn sounded, startling me a little, but I relaxed again. After all, what else was I going to do?

Hard objects began colliding with my hanging breasts. Then fingers. Then full hands grabbed me, but not in a sensual way. Fingers grazed the surface underneath my head. Slight vibrations reached my body when they were close, but it seemed they headed in all sorts of directions. Then one hand found its way to the opening around my hips. As though I was just an arcade game, these fingers felt me up, then pulled on the string like they were opening a set of blinds.

I flinched as the small device slid out of me in one fell swoop.

Then, as the porn soundtrack continued, I did

45

my best to relax and somehow enjoy the rushed contacts I got, but when an eager hand started fingering me as though he was looking for loose change in his car's ashtray compartment, I couldn't say I enjoyed it. But at least the previous event had warmed me up, so my natural lube had made the experience a bit more bearable.

And then the porn music ended, which meant that this third game was finally over.

Thankfully.

JUNICHI ESCORTED me to the next area.

The wide room contained twenty white pods that looked like giant eggs resting on their side, each on their own platforms.

As expected, the other women and I were instructed to yet again pick a pod.

This time, I want to be front and center! There has to be some meshing again. I want to see the rest of these contestants! If they are to objectify me and the rest of the women here, I deserve to see their naked bodies up close and personal. I want to enjoy the view for once. Maybe I'll even get to see Blondie?

So, I walked to the pod closest to the line that had been painted on the floor, and Junichi followed me.

It has to be their starting point for the next game, no?

Once we reached the pod, he lifted a rounded door and told me to get in.

I climbed up the three steps leading to the pod and looked in: it was smaller than I thought it'd be. It was also much wider than it was high.

"How am I supposed to sit in this?" I asked Junichi.

"You won't be sitting. Kneel, then lean forward, with your face toward that meshing," he said, pointing away from the area I was hoping to get a good view on. "Get in fetal position."

So much for my plan.

I got into child pose, with my arms next to me, extended backward, my back rounded and relaxed. The bottom of my enclosure was actually very comfortable, once again padded with thick memory foam. A few slots enabled air to come in and out, but the view from those only covered the floor right below me. Through the meshing, I could only see the pod closest to me.

"Move back until your behind touches the pod," Junichi said.

I scooted back as far as I could, and his hands gently prompted me to realign my hips so I pointed a bit more toward the left.

"You're good. This game has an emergency

stop. It involves regular sex and anal sex. If the contestant is being too violent with you, you press that big button in front of you, and he'll be disqualified. Do you understand?" he asked.

I moved my right hand toward the front, so it'd be ready, should I need to stop it.

"Don't press it unless you're sure."

"Okay, I get it."

"Good. I'll see you after the game. Warm yourself up a bit if you want." He closed the cover, and I heard him walk away.

I traced the outline of the emergency button, just in case I would have to use it, but I hoped I wouldn't. After all, I'd had anal sex before. But then again, there was the black man I'd seen earlier. Even his limp shaft was humongous. Anal sex with him could hurt.

I slid a hand between my legs and caressed myself in my darkened pod. A bit of light came in from the meshing and air slots below me, but not enough for me to see anything.

Then, while I was still busy with my warm up, the porn soundtrack began again.

A mere minute later, a panel slid open behind me.

Please don't be the black man, please don't be the black man.

First, it was a tip, and I kept praying. Then, a regular-sized cocked penetrated my pussy.

Thank you!

Gentle fingers feathered their way to my anus. Then something small poked its way past the entrance while he continued fucking my pussy. My anus closed again, although he hadn't retrieved what he'd put in. *Beads?* But for the first time in this game, I was at the mercy of a gentle lover. It almost felt normal, save for the egg pod I was restricted in.

An announcement was made in Japanese over the porn soundtrack, then the man came out of me. Whatever had been inserted in my ass was now dangling behind me. Angry shouts burst around the room in various languages. I only recognized an angry *Fuck* and *Hell no!*

What is going on?

Ten seconds later, my fuck fest resumed, and the man slowly inserted a second thing inside my ass, this one a bit bigger, but still manageable. His thrusts delighted me more and more and the added pressure from whatever he'd inserted in my ass improved the sensation. I moaned as he pushed a third, larger pearl up my ass. It made his dick feel thicker, fuller. The man behind me groaned and started pushing deeper into me. His cadence increased for a few seconds before it slowed right back down. He shouted something I didn't understand.

The unpredictable cadence of the man behind me disappointed me a little, it was smothering the inner fire that had been growing steadily in me until then.

What's going on?

Not being one who relied solely on others for pleasure, I slid a hand between my legs and toyed with my clit. Nobody said anything about penalties in this game (other than hitting the emergency button).

Maybe he saw my fingers, maybe he didn't, but he resumed a more satisfying cadence. I instantly forgave him for whatever had temporarily distracted him when he inserted the fourth bead into me. I definitely felt the large spherical shape on that one. My accompanying moan sounded loudly in my pod. As if I deserved a reward, a fifth bead got pushed into my ass. I was in heaven. The man was pounding me hard and fast now. I was on the brink as I'd never felt so full before. Just as I was about to come, my back instinctively pushed up against the top of my pod, but it was locked and I had nowhere to go.

How I wanted to feel that man's touch on my breasts, on my stomach, on my ass.

This game was both pleasant and disappointing.

Then, the beads and the man's cock retracted, much too fast for my liking, but it was no reason for pressing the emergency button. After all, he had brought me to the edge of ecstasy.

While loud moans and groans—both male and female—echoed all around the room, adding to the existing soundtrack, I continued to flick my clit until I reached climax and released the pressure that had been building up in me from the moment these games began.

I let out a long sigh of relief and cupped my hand over my throbbing pussy. My pounding heart sounded louder than normal in the privacy of my pod, and images of the blond stranger danced in my head.

Maybe it was him behind me just now?

"WOMEN WILL NOW TAKE THE LEAD," said Junichi as he helped me out of my pod.

He'd brought with him a white, short-sleeved shirt and a red pleated skirt on a hanger. No bra, but Junichi had also carried with him huge white panties. I slipped those on first. They were so big they could almost be called granny panties, except they didn't go as high. They simply covered a lot more ass than I was used to.

Then I put on the skirt. Junichi had my measurements from before and it was no doubt a skirt that had been chosen for me. The waist fit perfectly, but I couldn't bring it lower than my belly button. Thankfully, the pleated design allowed for my ample hips but the length didn't really work for me. The lower part of my ass was hanging out.

I turned to Junichi. "Do you have a longer skirt?" I asked.

He motioned for me to spin around. "No, it's fine. That's the length we need."

I nodded and put on the shirt.

Once again, Junichi had elected the smallest size I could have fit in. My breasts pushed against the fabric, the top two buttons barely kept me in. The shirt had a red piece of fabric that followed the neckline, and I tied it into a bow, which effectively covered the buttons that threatened to pop.

To complete the outfit, I put on the pair of red stilettos he'd also brought for me.

1:45 A.M.

FOR THE NEXT GAME, we were taken to a backstage area so cold I could almost see my breath. The now familiar porn soundtrack played loudly behind the walls of the next set.

Junichi told me the rules for the game that was about to begin. "You'll run into the next room and select a column. Each has a few holes around it. Pick a hole and place your mouth on it. If the pole turns red, that means you didn't find the right hole. Pick another one and try again, until the pole turns green. Then, lick, suck, use your hands, or do whatever you want to please the man inside the column, but when the light turns yellow, you have to stop. Do you understand?"

I nodded.

"Then, once it turns yellow, run out of the room as fast as you can. It's a timed event. Clear?"

"Yeah," I said, nodding again.

"Good luck." He left me alone with the rest of the women contestants.

I rubbed my arms to warm up a little and get rid of my goosebumps. My nipples poked through my shirt but there wasn't much I could do about that. *That's probably the effect they want anyway...*

Once all the assistants had left our group, a loud Japanese voice boomed over the speaker. Then a loud buzzer sounded and we ran into the room. My breasts bounced within the confines of the shirt as I made my way toward one of the available columns. Not surprisingly, porn movies were being projected onto every available surface, including the columns.

The one I picked was about three feet wide, and around it, about six or seven black holes peppered the surface. They ranged from knee-height to shoulder-height. I picked the one directly in front of me. A second later, the background onto which the porn movie aired turned red. I moved clockwise and selected the one about hip-height. I paused in place; the column stayed red. I moved to the third one, this one very low, forcing me to kneel on the floor. I waited for a second; the surface turned green.

What now?

But before I remembered the rest of Junichi's instructions, a hard cock appeared. It was pink, with a pronounced kink toward the left, and a big vein on top. After licking its salty length and wrapping my fist around its base, I started to bob on my mystery man. I sucked and sucked, enjoying the man's warm girth in my mouth. For once, I controlled every aspect of it, and I relished in that fact: no hands to push it too deep against the back of my throat and make me gag. The tiled floor was hard on my knees, so I readjusted quickly. I took my mouth off it for a second but kept going with one hand as the other cleared a tiny rock that had somehow wedged itself under my knee cap.

A second later, my mouth was back on the man's dick, my tongue twirled around its tip while my fist went up and down his shaft. I sucked on the tip and was about to take him in deeper when the column turned yellow.

I let go of him, and he instantly retracted into his hole.

I got up and ran back the way I'd come in until I'd left the set. I joined the other three women that had already gotten out, and we waited in silence for the others to be done.

A few minutes later, once all of the female

contestants had finished the current game, the porn soundtrack stopped, and our assistants came back to meet us.

Junichi walked up to me with a large Ziploc bag. "Please take off your panties and put them in here," he asked.

Can these games get any weirder?

The rest of the women were either talking to their assistants or taking off their panties.

No point questioning it.

I obeyed and slid them down my legs, seeing the large wet spot I'd left. I placed them in the bag Junichi was holding. He sealed the zipper-like opening then took the transparent bag away to God knows where.

Are panty vending machines a real thing?

A FEW MINUTES LATER, our group was escorted to the next set.

Unlike the others before, the walls here weren't white, so I could only assume no porn movie would be projected during this game. This room was nearly all mirrors. But there were a few spots that weren't reflecting light: several black circles at various heights around the room, some were about one foot from the floor, others up to two and a half.

We were instructed to stand in line and Junichi approached me to whisper instructions in my ear.

"There will be a timer counting down from 10 to 0. You need to pick a hole and line yourself up in time. Then, if you're lucky, the hole will open and a man will penetrate you. If not, you'll have to run to another hole with a man behind it and line yourself up. The goal of the game is to have twenty-five full thrusts. Not twenty-four, not twenty-six. Once you have twenty-five, you run back to this line here. The event is timed."

"You mean I need to let the dick come out of me each time?"

"No, you don't have to. But for the thrusts to count, they can't be shallow. You need to touch the wall every time, then almost let the man out of you as you move forward. Do you understand?"

I nodded and he walked out of the set.

A short while later, the rest of the assistants were also gone and the porn soundtrack started airing again.

About twenty seconds passed before the Japanese announcer spoke, then a gong sounded. I started running toward one of the holes, but slowed right down because running on a mirrored surface in high heels was plain dangerous. Once I got closer to one of the black holes, I tried to see if anything was visible through it. *Nothing.*

I walked over to the next one. All were made of the same black felt fabric. They looked identical except they weren't all at the same height.

The timer on the large display in the middle of the room was still counting down: 5... 4...

I picked the nearest hole and moved my pussy down until I no longer felt the cool mirrored surface, but the soft felt instead. My feet were shoulder-width apart, nearly a foot from the wall behind me, my knees slightly bent. All in all, it wasn't uncomfortable.

1... 0.

The gong rang again and I could have sworn I heard a sliding noise right behind my ass.

Across the room from me, I saw a few unattended cocks popping into the room. The woman standing directly in front of me had a priceless expression on her face as her body jerked. Had her eyes opened any more, they surely would have rolled out of their orifices.

The woman next to me went to an available cock that had just appeared.

Should I leave and line myself up with one of them?

But just as the thought came to me, a thick shaft pushed into me slowly, confirming I did hear something before. I bent forward some more, then moved my ass away from the mirrored wall, feeling him slide out of my wet pussy. I pulled away slowly —unsure how long he was—until he nearly fell out of me. I reached between my legs to keep him at the right angle, then I pushed back until my ass flattened against the wall.

2...

I did my best to concentrate on counting thrusts as opposed to enjoying them.

3... 4...

But ignoring the sensations brewing and growing inside me was near impossible. I started counting aloud to prevent losing track.

As I tallied each delicious slide up and down the mystery pole behind me, moans echoed all around the room: some sounded a bit like cats being strangled all the way to bestial grunts.

"12... 13... 14..."

I'd settled into a rhythm now, but my body was aching to reach gratification.

"20... 21... 22..." I could feel my legs weakening. *So.* "23..." *Damn.* "24..." *Close.*

I rammed my ass on the wall on the 25th thrust, and then debated whether I should put in a few more. I was so close... But women around me were already running toward the finish line and my competitive spirit kicked in, pulling me away from the wall and that wonderful mystery cock.

I can always finish myself off.

BUT THE NEXT event followed immediately thereafter, leaving me no time to release my built-up desires.

Here's to hoping the next game will do the trick.

The moment we stepped into the next room, it felt like we'd entered a hot and humid jungle, except there were no trees, no animals. It was just a small, brightly illuminated room. Like fog lights, each beam coming down from the ceiling cut through the thick mist that filled the air.

Beads of condensation began trickling down my face, my back, my front, my legs. But the trickle soon made my entire skin glisten and ooze with sweat. My white shirt was now transparent and sticking to my breasts. I tried undoing a button, but it didn't do anything to cool me off. The blonde woman next to me tried to vent herself, but her shirt just clamped onto her skin as though it was a wet swimsuit.

There was no cool or dry air in this room.

Even the act of breathing became laborious, which made the room spin around me. I sat down... Or I may have fallen onto the floor instead.

A moment later, Junichi brought me a tall glass of water with ice. I let it rest on my cheeks for a second before gulping it down and nearly choking on the ice cube. Then, as if the universe had listened to my silent prayers, a large door opened, which let a burst of cooler air in, dropping the humidity levels down. Way down.

I handed my empty glass to Junichi and he left.

Over the next few minutes, the roller-coaster of climates continued, with really cold air now taking over the room. The dampness of my shirt turned it into a refreshing attribute. And it helped bring my senses back. I was now able to stand up again.

And finally, after the climate problem had sorted itself out, bringing the room to a normal and slightly cool temperature, an announcement was made in Japanese.

Junichi reappeared next to me and translated the instructions: "Pick one of the open tunnels. It will be dark. Crawl on all fours until you come across a couple of bowls on the floor. This is where you'll stop. Look up and tease those balls until the man gets hard. You're not allowed to touch his penis or they'll deduct points. You're limited to testicles, anus, and the area in between. Your tools will be your fingers, tongue, ice, and a warming gel."

"That's it?"

"It's a timed event. And you can get bonus points if you get both testicles in your mouth at once. Good luck!" he said.

I looked around and stood in front of one of the openings I now noticed. A few women were still with their assistants.

Once everyone was ready, a loud buzzer sounded. I got down on my hands and knees then entered the tunnel I'd chosen.

As expected, it was dark, but for now, I could still see a little light coming from the room I'd just left. I saw the tunnel make a left turn a few feet in front of me. My limbs went as fast as they could on the cool metal surface. Thankfully, it felt solid, not like a hanging vent that my own weight could make crash onto a floor below.

As soon as I made the corner though, I lost the faint light I previously had, forcing me to slow down and feel my way so I wouldn't bang my head on a wall. Little by little, I advanced until I finally touched a bowl. (It'd be more accurate to say that I inadvertently pushed and toppled it.) But feeling my way around, I found it again and realized it had a lid on. I brought it back next to the other bowl and remove both lids. One had cold ice cubes, the other a tube of something. It had to be the warming gel Junichi had talked about.

I looked up. Thankfully, my eyes were starting to get used to the darkness.

This part of the tunnel was much higher than the previous part. I sat down—the cool metal nearly shocked my exposed, wet pussy—and that's when I noticed something dangling above me. I reached up and my hand landed on one very long, limp dick. A loud buzzer sounded above me.

Yeah, can't touch it, but can't wait to see what he'll turn into once excited.

I reached higher until I felt the ceiling of sorts, then went looking for the man's balls. I had no idea which way he was positioned. But I soon found the clean-shaven sack hanging above me. It seemed small compared to his accompanying cock.

I folded my legs and rested my wet pussy upon my ankles.

The air was stale in the tunnel and I could smell

my own arousal. I placed an ice cube in my mouth and let it melt a little, helping to cool off my urges as well. Then, with my cold tongue, I teased his balls. The temperature difference made them go up, then I grabbed them both and sucked on them. Both fit in my mouth, along with the ice cube. His dick twitched, his balls tightened and moved up some more, but I kept sucking on them until the ice was no more.

I spread warming gel on his balls with my fingers and blew on them, which made his testicles return to a more relaxed, slightly lower position. I began massaging his balls gently. I even spread some of that gel toward his anus, then got another ice cube in my mouth and repeated the process.

The man's dick grew both in girth and length. It was just beautiful... and irresistible.

I wrapped my hands around it. I wanted to feel its veins carving their unique signature onto the otherwise straight shaft.

An alarm sounded above me, but I opened my mouth as wide as I could to swallow the man's tip. There was simply nothing else that could fit. I sucked on it, my fingertips not even close to touching each other as I tried to wrap them around his girth. Red lights flashed all around me. I once again chose to ignore the alarm. I didn't care anymore. I was competitive like any other person, but I simply couldn't ignore that dick.

If I flip myself around, maybe I can push my pussy onto the tip of it?

Can I lift my hips high enough?

Worth a try.

I took my mouth away from his beautiful cock, and he disappeared instantly.

His dangling balls, his beautiful cock, all of it had retracted up past the slot in the ceiling... and the trap had closed again.

I heard Junichi's voice in the distance. "You can come back out now."

I've been cock-teased one too many times here.

My pussy now ached for real action.

My mind wanted real physical contact.

My heart... well, I couldn't care less what my heart wanted at that very moment.

MY ASSISTANT REPEATED the instructions again:

"Select a seat, then sit facing the front or back. When the game starts, a remote will drop from above. Use the knobs and buttons as you see fit. The goal is to come at the same time as your partner. When you reach orgasm, you must pull on the remote, as though it was a chain. You are NOT allowed to talk."

I nodded then walked in the next room. As per most of the previous games, porn was being projected on the walls, with the accompanying soundtrack blazing loudly.

This room looked near empty, save for a dozen very low, mini pyramids that were coming up from indented grooves on the floor. As I got closer, I realized they were more like mini-volcanoes, but with rounded, indented craters.

As ordered, I walked to one of the contraptions and straddled it, my bent knees positioned in the moat-like indent that surrounded it. Instantly, I realized the crater wasn't round, but oval, so I realigned myself so my pussy and ass were positioned correctly. A remote control lowered itself from above. I looked up. More strings dangled from various anchors above the set, each woman had already received their remote.

I got a hold of mine and inspected it. It had a large power button at the top, so I pressed it.

A second later, a slight breeze blew on my ass and pussy. My groin no longer rested on the previously hard surface of the crater. My legs were still anchored securely—although widely spread—on the rounded edges of the indented volcano.

Then, someone penetrated me from behind. At first, it was just something small—a finger?—then his dick, which was nice, although I would have preferred him in my pussy instead, especially after having seen that large cock in the last game. My pussy desperately craved some pumping action, and from something worth feeling.

Just as the thought crossed my mind, I had a

second look at the remote. I pressed an unmarked purple button and my wish came true. *Kind of.* The dick that entered my pussy was bigger than the one in my ass. And it began vibrating. I looked down and saw a bright purple device, complete with life-like details. I wrapped my hand around the base below me and it felt soft and warm. I couldn't see who was handling it, just the person's hand.

He pulled it in and out of me in complete sync with his anal pumping action. This was the best torture in the world, and it made my entire body shiver. I knew I wouldn't be able to hold off very long. I tried to distract myself by having a third look at the remote. A brightly lit arrow flashed on the lower circular button. I moved my finger in an arc along the illuminated symbol and it reduced the intensity of the vibrations.

But even at the lowest setting, I was going to come any second. The man below me started thrusting harder, deeper. *Is he getting there too?* The intensity of his pounding had increased so much he actually pushed me off of my straddling position. I quickly re-seated myself before cranking up the speed on the vibrator. I could no longer control my body: I moaned and quivered with my eyes closed. I'd breached past the entrance and there was no turning back at this point. I quivered as I rode the wave of pleasure those games had triggered in me... then I remembered I had to do something. I reopened my eyes and I pulled on the string attached to the remote above me, and a huge bucket of icy cold water splashed down on me just as I reached the apex of my climax.

The finale would have been better without that... and if accompanied by the warm embrace of a man behind me, but it'd still been amazing.

The man pounded me a couple more times, then his warm juices exploded in my ass. A second later, he was gone, having pulled both his dick and the buzzing vibrator out of me.

I reached down between my legs and felt my pounding heartbeat through my swollen pussy. The crater had once again closed itself.

4:30 A.M.

AT THE END of the night, still a bit bewildered by what the special invitation had led to, but mostly pleased, I got changed back in my evening gown then slipped my participation prize in my purse: a hundred thousand yen. *Not bad!*

There hadn't been an award or closing ceremony at all.

I had no idea how points had been calculated or who had won the games. Then again, perhaps it was all a big scam, and nobody had gotten the grand prize, but at least I hadn't lost anything (assuming the video was to remain private).

Otherwise...

Heck, even if it goes public. Who cares? It was all good fun.

But as I was leaving the building, still lost in my thoughts, I spotted the handsome blond man about to get in one of the cabs that had been called for us.

"Hey, wait!" I called out as I hurried my pace toward him.

He turned to me, a confused frown on his face.

"Do you speak English?"

He shook his head. "No."

"*Français? ¿Español?*"

He shook his head again.

Is he going to be worth the trouble?

I pointed to him, then me, and then the cab.

He raised his shoulders, then nodded.

Does he think I just want to share a ride?

I stepped forward into his personal space and placed a hand on one of his hips, then looked him in the eyes, my mouth partly open.

Before I could overthink my actions, he'd planted his soft lips onto mine and wrapped his arms around my back. His ardent fervor added to my already kindled desires; I wanted to do him right there and then, but I resisted the urge and pulled back long enough to tilt my head toward the cab.

He nodded, took off his jacket, and we both slid onto the backseat.

I leaned forward to tell the cab driver my hotel address in English. The moment I was done speaking, Blondie pulled me back into his arms, and we resumed where we'd left off a few seconds earlier. *Well, almost.* He'd also taken hold of one of my breasts and his other hand had already worked its way to my knees, up my long flowing dress.

For a split second, I worried about offending the cab driver or creating some kind of cultural discomfort, but it had been too long of a night to waste my energy on that thought.

He can just look elsewhere, like toward the road ahead.

While my tongue mingled with Blondie's, my hands reached behind him. I untucked his shirt and let my hands slide up against his soft, warm back. I hadn't made out in a cab in so long, I'd forgotten how uncomfortable it was. But no matter the awkward positioning, after games that had involved too many faceless encounters, the warmth of his skin on my hands was invigorating. I couldn't wait to get the full-body experience.

And he seemed to share my eagerness.

His hand had already climbed to my thighs, which had raised the fabric of my dress as well. I parted my legs, rolling out a red-carpet invitation for his touch. His mouth pulled away from mine for a few seconds and I gently pushed on his jaw so I could meet his glance. In his steel-blue eyes flickered a hungry flame that flashed brighter than I'd ever seen.

By now, his fingers had breached the outline of my soaked thong. His soft lips zigzagged their way down from my earlobe to my chest bones, subjecting my neck to the perfect combination of sucks, licks, and gentle bites. My heart pounded hard and fast in my chest, but it was nothing compared to the throbbing going on between my legs.

Letting my head rest on the back of the car seat, I reveled in delight each time he caressed my skin with his soft, balmy kisses. I moved one of my hands to his head and let my fingers run through his thick, soft hair. He smelled of coconut and sea breeze; a deep inhalation of his cologne had me mentally transport our make-out session to the most exotic and private beach I'd ever been on...

But that's when the driver coughed loudly in his seat.

Blondie got off of me and I looked out the window. I recognized my hotel.

We're already here?

I pulled down my dress then fumbled around for my purse.

After digging out enough money for the fare and a tip, I exited the vehicle through the door that Blondie held open for me. I took the hand he offered and stepped out onto the curb.

5:00 A.M.

WE RUSHED into the empty lobby and headed toward the elevators. One was there already; its bell dinged the instant I pressed the call button.

After stepping into the small space, I pushed my floor number, and Blondie spun me around before locking lips with me.

He'd already pinned me against one of the mirrored walls by the time the door closed. The bulge in his pants dug into my stomach when he pressed his hard body against mine. My chest heaved, and our mouths devoured each other's while his hands held mine immobile on either side of my head. In a muted clunk, my purse dropped to the carpeted floor as we sped upward.

As though a magnetic pull somehow connected

our souls, my chest leaned forward. His lips headed down my cleavage while he kept me restrained. Desire and frustration mingled in my mind. I just wanted to lean into him, reach into his pants, ride his cock like it was the last one on earth.

The ding of the door sounded again when we reached my floor, so he let me go and walked out. But the fiery spark in his eyes and his loud exhalation made his intentions clear. I bent my knees to collect my fallen purse, and he offered his hand to help me up and out of the elevator.

And courteous?

I need to fuck this man right now!

I led him to my room, which was just a few doors down the left.

While I fumbled with my room card to get the green light I so desperately sought, he stood behind me, breathing deeply on the back of my neck. First, he lifted my dress up to my hips, then he pressed himself against my ass, his precious bulk poking my lower back, his hands resting on my waist, the flowing fabric of my dress piled on his forearms.

The green light finally appeared on the card reader, and I pushed open my door.

He'd slipped my dress up and over my head and arms even before the door softly closed behind us, granting us the privacy that hadn't existed earlier that night. Stepping backward in nothing but my heels and underwear, I pulled him toward my bed by his belt as I tried to undo it at the same time. He tossed his jacket toward the corner where my dress had landed a second earlier, then he undid the tiny black buttons of his white shirt.

When he exposed his chiseled chest, I pulled on his undone buckle and whipped his belt out of their loops. His waist button didn't stand a chance; it popped off its thread when I pulled on the waist of his dress pants.

A split second later, I fell backward on my bed —I'd forgotten how high it was—and Blondie landed on me, his lips munching at my neck. My hands found his zipper and undid it, setting free his manhood and drawing a huge smile on my lips.

How I love men who go commando. So fucking convenient.

He, too, had been clean shaved by those in charge of the games (or perhaps that was his regular 'do). I rolled my fingers around his girth. I admired its manly, majestic beauty for a second as he continued to pull down his pants.

Fuck. Where are my condoms when I need them?

While he fumbled with his shoes and pants, I rolled over to my side and reached into the small cosmetic bag on my nightstand. I found what I needed and unwrapped the first in the golden strip I'd brought with me.

As I attempted to roll over and reposition myself on my back, below him, he stopped me. His hands firmly on my hips, he flipped me on my stomach then pulled me back toward him; my limbs slid on the soft, silky comforter until my legs fell off of the end. He grabbed my ass, his fingers dug into my flesh as he caught me just before my knees crashed onto the floor below. He took the condom from my hand, then unrolled it on himself in record time.

A second later, he nudged my lacy thong off to the side, his fingers slid between my slick folds, and his cock thrust into me without further preamble.

Finally.

I swear a mystical creature had taken hold of my vocal cords at that point; there was no other way to explain the bestial roar that escaped my lips when my ass smacked against his warm skin. Each time he drove his hard cock deep into me, faster and faster, he took me up a few more notches. Physical nirvana was within reach. I arched my back, lifting my breasts up from the bed. I turned my head and caught a glance of him: his parted legs in a mid-squat position, his head tilted back, his mouth agape, his tongue in the corner of his lips, his grunts matching the cadence at which he was pounding me.

I let my heels find the floor below me, then straightened my legs, bringing my ass higher. He unfolded his height. Two of his digits traced a deep circle on my right butt cheek, then he cupped his hand and slapped me hard. Twice. Three times. I yelped on the fourth slap, but it morphed into a squeal as my pain merged with the blossoming orgasm that surged through my cells.

As though a perverted guardian angel had choreographed our encounter, he came into me just as my legs were about to let go. He pushed me forward in one final thrust. His warm chest landed on my back as I collapsed toward the pillows, my heart pounding, my pussy and soul finally satisfied.

WHEN I WOKE up a few hours later, Blondie had left.

No notes, no attempts at goodbye, nothing. Just a cold, empty spot on the other side of the bed.

The previous evening had proven itself to be entertaining—most certainly during its last stretch —but it hadn't fulfilled my deeper need for connection.

The games hadn't truly satisfied me, just like my self-induced orgasms had never really displayed that transcendent quality I knew to exist, even though I could count the instances I'd relished in it on only one hand. Something special, unique, almost unworldly happened when two people in love gazed into each other's eyes as they simultaneously reached their orgasmic apex.

For a few seconds, on those rare occasions, two truly could become one.

But it had been so long since I'd felt it.

In this lifetime, will I once again delight in such an exquisite, deep, and significant spiritual and physical experience?

Maybe not?

I let go of that depressing thought as I started packing my suitcase. I chose to think of something else—like last night's games, once more.

They'd mostly been about objectification. Some rich guy's perversion. I couldn't judge him for it because I wouldn't want anyone judging me for wanting what I wanted.

That being said, I had to admit that topic used to piss me off. Years ago, I'd get annoyed when a few members of an all-male construction crew whistled at a beautiful woman on the street. Now I knew my feelings had been hurt because they hadn't whistled *at me*.

When I look back in my figurative rearview mirror, seeing my path over the previous months, I think being objectified actually helped improve my struggling self-esteem.

Somehow...

Isn't it interesting how something not so good can be so useful in the big scheme of things?

But objectification had also led me to shallow, all-about-fun sex, which can be somewhat of a letdown after a while.

The more I think about it, the more I need to find something different. Something a little more meaningful, a little more compelling, a little more intimate. But I don't want to lose the progress I've made on the physical side.

There's gotta be a way, no?

But how...?

PART TWO

MY XXX EXPERIENCE

THE PLAN

CRAZY SHIT, I know! But it gets me every time. Talk about a hard night's work for my mystery stewardess.

My Japanese is non-existent, but I do know a lovely Japanese woman who recently started working with us, and I'd like to get to know her better. And maybe she can help me track down Sophia, or at least find a copy of that video.

So here are my options:

OPTION 1: Track down Mr. Suzuki.

I still don't know what airline Sophia works for (so I don't know which manifests to hunt down), but

I Googled his last name, and it is the second most popular family name in all of Japan.

Likelihood of success: Nil.

OPTION 2: Find a copy of the game show.

It was obviously recorded, but no matter how hard I searched for it online, I couldn't locate a copy. During my travels, I've seen countless Asian street markets overflowing with manga porn and various ripped-off copies of movies, games, and comic books. I may be able to find a copy of that video in person.

Likelihood of success: Low to average.

OPTION 3: Track down Junichi.

I also Googled his name, thinking that if it were unique enough, I'd stand a chance to find him. But it's a very common given name for boys.

Likelihood of success: Nil.

The second option is the only viable one, and I've got an upcoming trip to Japan, so it works perfectly for me.

Now, let's hope my cute Japanese stewardess will be helpful in more ways than one.

WHAT HAPPENED

WOULDN'T YOU KNOW IT, my plan was off to a great start.

And I didn't even have to try.

Within the first two minutes of meeting Ms. Keiki Yamamoto during the pre-flight meeting, I knew luck was once again going to be on my side.

"I heard about you," she said. "Your reputation with the female crew..."

Is this a joke? Is she part of some secret program put together by the airline to ensure I don't harass women?

"What did you hear?" I asked her in a voice low enough that she'd be the only one to hear me.

From my breast pocket to my navel, she slid a finger down my shirt. She poked her manicured nail behind my belt, pulling me in closer to her.

"They say you're a well-endowed machine worth testing out." She pointed for me to lean down toward her. She whispered the rest in my ear. "I heard a test run is all women get with you. But it's a highly-recommended test run."

Well if that isn't the best compliment a man can get, I don't know what is.

"Interesting. Curious to find out first-hand?" I asked quietly, my eyes locked onto hers.

She didn't budge, but simply continued with the same daring expression in her eyes. "Maybe we can test each other when we land?"

"Possibly," was all I said, but I followed it with my winning smile and a wink.

She was putty in my hands and she knew it.

She broke eye contact and looked down.

So, it was with my mind in the gutter and high hopes of an entertaining layover that I embarked on my journey to NRT/Tokyo.

AS PREVIOUSLY AGREED, Keiki met me in the lobby of the hotel a few hours after we had checked in.

I was sipping a cold Kirin while waiting for her, hoping she'd wear something short that would expose more of her beautiful skin. But she joined me at the bar in a pair of skin-tight jeans, platform shoes, and a purple, short-sleeved turtleneck that hugged her small breasts. I offered to buy her a drink, but she turned me down, so I quickly emptied my own glass, settled my bill, and then we stepped out of the lobby to hail a taxi.

When she slid in the backseat just ahead of me, the tiny ass in her jeans still left plenty for my lazy imagination. She said something in Japanese to the cab driver before turning her attention to me. "We're going to the best night market I know. Can you tell me more about the movie you're looking for so I can help you find it?"

I told her everything I knew. No point in being sly or shy about it. I divulged every detail I'd memorized from my stewardess's description of the games.

She stroked my arm with her delicate fingers. "You're as naughty as they say you are... Will you let me watch those sex games with you?" The eyeliner she'd applied only serve to highlight the longing in her eyes.

"I'm sure that could be arranged."

I leaned in toward her, my hand on the side of her silky black hair, and I let my thumb caress her cheek. She bit her red-hot lips. As though my eyes were hypnotized by her shiny lipstick, I dove into her vanilla-scented space and kissed her. First, it was just a brush of the lips, but it evolved into something more eager, hungrier. I teased her with my tongue, and her response only served to light things up between us. My dick reacted by pushing up against the fabric of my jeans, so I readjusted, tucking the tip behind my belt for now.

We reached our destination too soon for my taste, which put an end to our friendly cab interlude. Keiki pulled away from me when the driver cleared his throat, which preceded some exchange in Japanese.

We got out, and I paid the fare once Keiki translated the amount for me.

My gorgeous, petite friend led me by the hand through a maze of smaller streets until we reached a busy night market, which had me recalibrate my definition of the word *crammed*. If she hadn't been holding my hand, I could have easily lost Keiki in the crowd here. And she was a fast walker that one... Surprisingly so, especially with her platform shoes on. I couldn't wait to see her ass out of those jeans.

Around us, the stands we passed sold everything: fresh sashimi, comic books, running shoes, cheap accessories, backpacks, noodles, loose teas and herbs, underwear, socks, puzzles, and way too many random-looking snacks to count. Smells piled on top of one another, resulting in something intriguing yet mouth-watering.

We weaved through the thick crowd and stopped at the first stand that sold movies. Among the long string of words that came out of the exchange between Keiki and the shop attendant a couple of feet away from me, I overheard Suzuki a few times. *That's a good sign, no?*

She walked back toward me. "The man says he doesn't have this particular movie, but he knows another merchant here who could arrange to find it for you."

"Do you know where the other merchant is located?"

She returned to the man and their exchange continued in Japanese. The man's hands pointed toward different directions as he spoke.

Then she was back by my side, pulling on my hand to get me going. "I know where to find it now. Let's go."

I smiled at the helpful man and followed Keiki toward my prize.

About ten minutes and three street blocks later, we paused our crowd-weaving in front of another stand that carried lots of movies and manga.

"I'll talk to the man and find out," Keiki said as she let go of my hand.

"Great, thanks. I'll stay here and browse through his selection."

The assortment of DVDs, CDs, and VCDs didn't appear to be sorted in any comprehensible manner. Interspersed together were music CDs, children's anime, Hollywood classics, and hard-core porn. I randomly picked up one of the cardboard sleeves wrapped in plastic. On it were three

Japanese school girls in their uniforms, on their knees, hands tied at the wrists in front of them, their mouths wide open, tears running down their cheeks.

What the fuck is this?

I flipped the cover over to expose a naked man seen from behind, a whip dangling from one of his hands.

What?

I put it down, shaking my head. I flipped through more of the covers, until my eyes caught sight of a professional woman in a dress, half of it undone, one of her beautiful, augmented breasts fully exposed. Her smile was what I'd expect from a stock photo. I flipped the cover over. Several thumbnails competed for my attention: one of her squirting a jet out of her blurred-out pussy, another series of thumbnails next to each other where she straddled a man, staring at the camera, almost in a tutorial kind of way. Then a few more thumbnails of her ass and tits, fully exposed.

By now, Keiki had reappeared by my side. "He knows someone who knows someone... If you're willing to pay 100,000 yen, he'll find a copy for you tonight."

"What's that?" I asked her.

"Like 800 or 900 dollars?"

While I didn't expect to find my stewardess's video in a discount bin, the man's price seemed a bit steep.

"Can we tell him we'll think about it and see if other stands would have a copy?"

"I doubt anyone else would. Based on some of the people involved, you're lucky to even be granted this chance."

"What people?"

She shook her head. "Nobody you'd know."

"Okay then. Tell him I'll take it. When can he have it for me?"

She lifted her finger in the air, then returned to chat with the man who was staring at me in a way that made my spine shiver.

What's his problem?

But Keiki had already resumed talking with him, and that creepy sensation dissolved just as fast as it had appeared.

She was back by my side within a few seconds. "Give him half now, then he'll write down the address where we can pick up the copy and pay the other half. You have your computer with you to watch it?"

"Sure, I've got my laptop. Does giving him half the money now seem weird to you?"

She stared me down. "And you buying a pirated copy of a private video isn't weird? ...Or illegal?"

"Good point." I dug my wallet out and handed her ten purplish 5,000-yen bills. "Wait," I said as she was about to walk toward the man again, my money in hand. "I'll get this movie too. How much is it?" I asked her.

"The sign says 2,000 yen each."

I pulled two blue bills out of my wallet and handed them to her along with what I hoped would be an entertaining movie.

I watched the transaction happen from a distance. He wrote down something on a piece of paper and then handed it to her, with both his hands.

She came back to me and handed me my purchase wrapped in an unmarked plastic bag. She pulled on my hand again. "Come on. Let's go. We'll meet someone close to our hotel in two hours. We'll give him the rest of the money and he'll hand you what you want."

SOMETHING SOMEWHERE HAD ALTERED the vibe between Keiki and me, and I couldn't put my finger on it. Of course, the cab ride back suffered because of that mysterious thing.

We did have two hours to kill, and while I couldn't think of a better way to spend it then getting her naked and humping, I no longer thought she was in the mood for it.

"So, you're not going to tease me about my purchase?" I asked, lifting my bag in the air and hoping it would trigger a desire for some mutual fun.

She stayed silent for a while, shaking her head. "You like big breasts?" she finally asked.

"No, I'm not picky. I like ALL breasts. Small, medium, large, real, fake..."

Her lips drew a faint smile.

"I'm sure you have gorgeous breasts," I said.

"I know I do."

Is her vibe switching again?

"I'd like to see them... Just so I can fulfill that original request you had for me before we flew here."

"Are you hungry?" she asked as the driver slowed down in front of our hotel.

I dug in my jeans to retrieve my wallet. "Depends on what you have in mind..."

She insisted on paying the fare, so I let her.

"Ramen noodles okay with you?" she asked.

That damn vibe hasn't switched.

"Fine," I said, doing my best to hide my disappointment.

She walked into a busy restaurant and found two empty seats next to each other at the bar.

"What do you want?" she asked me.

I had no idea what my options even were. "I'll get the same as you."

She ordered, and then I confronted her.

"So, what's up? Did I do something wrong?"

"No. Yes. No."

Just like all women I'd ever met in my life had

managed to do, she already had me confused. "Which is it? Did I do something you didn't like?"

"Not directly."

"Then what is it?"

"I'm nervous about the people we'll meet," she said.

"People? I thought you said we'd meet one person?"

"I don't know. I've never ever been in contact with those kinds of people."

"What do you mean?"

"The man who recorded that video..."

"Mr. Suzuki?" I asked.

"Shhh... Don't say his name." She looked around us, as though I'd just insulted someone important.

"But isn't it like saying Mr. Johnston or Mr. James? A name that's not particularly rare?"

"Let's call him Mr. James then. This particular, very wealthy Mr. James isn't someone you want to mess with."

"Isn't he just a regular rich guy?"

She looked around again before speaking, and when she did, her voice was so low I had to lean toward her to hear her words. "He didn't get wealthy by legal means."

"Video contraband?"

"You'd wish it was that."

I lowered my voice as well, and this time I leaned to whisper in her ear. "What is it then? Drugs? Weapons?"

She cupped her hand next to my ear to speak. "Much worse than that."

But before I could ask her more questions, our steaming bowls of noodle soup sat in front of us.

"Let's forget about it and enjoy our food," she said.

11:15 P.M.

AFTER I PAID for our meal, I double-checked my wallet to see if I had enough money for the upcoming transaction that had Keiki so worried. I definitely didn't want to make things worse by accidentally swindling the guy or guys who'd be trading with us.

"Time to go," she said, looking at the clock on the wall.

"I'm ready. Please lead the way."

She held on to my hand again as we walked around the block. And this was no sexy hand holding that promised a happy ending; this was the hand of a young girl looking to be reassured.

The more we walked, the more I psyched myself up. I'd always been a man's man and I was ready to deal with whatever man or men Mr. Suzuki would send to meet us. Cultural differences be damned.

"We're here," she said, looking up at a noodle shop that looked very similar yet different from the one we'd eaten at only minutes ago.

That's where criminals trade contraband in Japan?

"Let me go in," I said.

"That's silly. You don't even speak Japanese."

"Good point. At least let me go in with you."

"Okay," she said, nodding vehemently as we entered the noodle shop.

As I was about to whisper a question in her ear, a short, skinny man approached us and said something in Japanese.

She bowed, answered, and then nodded to me.

I took out my wallet and handed out the stash of pre-counted bills I'd located in their own compartment.

He handed me a small USB stick. Not what I expected, but hey, movies can be saved on a stick instead of a DVD. I certainly didn't want to risk offending him, so I let it slide. But what I didn't understand was why Keiki and he were still talking.

He's got his money. I've got a copy of my game show. What's the holdup here?

The man handed Keiki a small black bag. I had

no idea what he was telling her, but I saw fear in her eyes.

She nodded profusely, bowed to the man, and then pulled me by the elbow as she rushed out of the restaurant.

She kept looking behind us as we hurried back to our hotel.

"What's going on?" I asked.

All I got was a shake of the head. And her head kept shaking until we made it back to the safety and privacy of my room.

"WHAT'S GOING ON?" I repeated as I framed her petite body between my arms, locking eyes with her. "What did he say? What did he give you?"

"Don't worry about it. It's my problem."

"No! I obviously got you involved in whatever this is. I'll help you get out of it. Tell me what I can do."

She snaked her way out of my arms, then headed to the mini-fridge. She opened it. "A drink will help. Go get us some ice, please?"

She handed me the empty plastic bucket from the top of the fridge.

"As long as you promise to stay here," I said, agreeing against my will. "I'll be right back."

I hurried down the hall, unable to find the ice

machine at first, but when I walked by the staircase, I saw a sign that read "Ice machine 10th floor".

By the time my bucket was filled and I'd walked back to my door, I saw Keiki waiting outside of my room, the door barely ajar behind her.

"Don't close it! I left my room key on the desk."

She moved her index finger to her lips and then motioned for me to come closer. When I reached her, she whispered in my ear. "We'll share a drink, you'll watch your movie, then you'll call me. Once you're done with whatever this game show is, I'll need you to take me. On your bed. I'll need you to be rough, rip my clothes off, tie me up. I'll try to fight you, I'll attempt to yell. I'll pretend to not enjoy it... I may even cry, but I'll be loving every moment of it. Understood?"

This woman deserves a prize for flip-flopping.

"What? Why not now?" I asked, placing my hands on her hips and moving into her space.

"I want you to enjoy your game show first. After all, this is what you really wanted, no?"

"Yes... But who's to say you won't change your mind or fall asleep before I finish watching it?

"Don't worry, I won't. I promise."

I certainly didn't want to risk it. "Wanna watch it with me?" I asked.

"No, I've got something else to do. Call my room the moment you're done watching it.

I met her eyes and only saw truth in what she was saying.

"Why are you telling me all of this now then?"

"Because I don't want to explain what I want you to do to me just before you do it."

I guess that makes sense?

While I wasn't particularly into what she suggested, it could be hot. Especially if she was into it. Maybe those violent Japanese porn movies were actually based on real popular fetishes.

"Should we have a safe word or something?"

"Probably."

"Probably is the safe word?" I asked, confused as hell.

"No, I don't know. Think of something."

And, whether it was because I was in Japan or because I was exhausted after running around, the only word that came to mind was ridiculous. "Samurai?" I suggested.

She raised her shoulders. "Fine by me."

"But if I decide to cover your mouth so you can't scream and get us kicked out of the hotel, how will I know I've gone too far?"

She raised her shoulders again. "Don't worry. You won't."

KEIKI OPENED the door and took the ice bucket from my hands. "Can you make me a drink, please?" she asked.

"Sure. What's your poison?" I opened the mini-fridge.

"Whiskey on the rocks."

That woman was something. Hard to follow, but definitely *something*.

I dropped two ice cubes into one of the two glass tumblers on my desk, then dumped the contents of one mini-bottle into it before grabbing and opening a can of beer for myself. I carried her glass over to her. "Here you go, Keiki."

"Cheers," she said, clinking her glass against my can and winking at me.

She reached for the USB stick I'd left on the corner of the desk earlier.

"So, this is the game show you needed to find so badly..."

"I hope it is," I said, taking it from her hand. "Do you think they ripped us off?"

"Don't think so. Put it in your computer and see?"

I unpacked my laptop, placed it on the desk, and then turned it on. After taking a seat on the chair, I inserted the stick into one of my USB ports. I sipped my beer while the stick's red light started flashing.

A few seconds later, my computer had recognized it, and I clicked my way to the files listed on the drive. Among a bunch of extensions I didn't recognize, I saw an .mp4 file called "Sex Games".

I double-clicked it and a large window opened, showing large Japanese characters.

"What does this say?" I asked Keiki.

"Private Sex Games."

The screen had moved to something else, with lots of text.

"And this?"

"This video is private... blah blah blah, cannot be copied... You know. *That* screen."

I nodded and then the movie began with naked men running on a game show set.

"This is it!" I said.

She stood up. "Then that's my cue to get out."

"You sure you don't want to watch it with me? Maybe there are some things I'll need you to translate? Or maybe we can make things a bit more interactive?"

She tilted her head and pursed her lips. "I'm sure you'll understand all of it. I think you've got a busy evening ahead of you." She walked up to me, downed the last sip of her drink, and then kissed me. "But you MUST call me the instant you're done watching it. I want to hear all about it. You know my room number."

Her lips lingered on mine some more, my hands went up to grab her ass, but she walked away from me.

"Later," she promised with a wink.

And with that, she exited my room, her tiny rump still as enticing as ever.

I could imagine a thousand ways to reward Keiki for her helpful work tonight. She'd get my porn-Oscar-worthy performance soon enough. Violent and all, if that was what she wanted.

But what did that scrawny man tell her that had her so worried?

And I didn't know what had happened while I'd gone to fetch ice... She seemed much more relaxed when I got back.

But I killed those thoughts. I had something much more important to take care of right now: I had to work on identifying Sophia.

I walked into the bathroom, took off my clothes, and then put on the lush bathrobe the hotel had provided. A box of tissues and my carry-on size of lube in hand, I sat in front of my computer and began watching the games, the red light of my expensive USB drive still flashing.

AFTER A FEW MORE SHOTS OF naked men running on various sets, a quick screen transition fit for an original Batman fight scene (in Japanese) flashed on my screen. Then, two columns of five animated GIFs appeared; they reminded me of porn-site thumbnails. On the left: five limp dicks; on the right: five erect ones. The commentator said something in Japanese, then, about ten seconds later, blue diagonal lines were traced between the two columns, using the same technology a sports commentator would use to explain a play—except that limp and erect junk was matched.

What is this shit show?

After a short, erotically themed interlude that consisted of various women coming together in vocal harmony, a large headline popped onto the screen, followed by the first hint of English: *GAME 1*.

A wide shot of several male contestants standing in line served as background for whatever the Japanese commentator needed to go on about. Based on the visual symbols popping up on the screen, I could only assume he was providing instructions for this first game. The cartoon-like images reminded me of what my buddies and I used to doodle in the margins of our books when bored in high school: artful but childlike-drawings by horny boys.

At first overly circular boobs were drawn, then two stick figures were added. An arrow was drawn from one man to one boob, then a second arrow from the other man to the other boob.

The screen got wiped clean of the initial drawings, then an erection was drawn in white ink. Whoever was drawing over the screen traded his white pen for a red one, then wrapped the erect dick in a circle, then traced a diagonal line across it. *No erection allowed?*

Below it, a downward arrow and ¥10000 flashed on the screen. *Is that a penalty?*

Then a timer icon appeared. While I hadn't gotten any of what the fast-talking Japanese man had been going on about for the past couple of minutes, I believed I'd at least gotten the gist of the rules.

After another short transition with a "3... 2... 1... Go" countdown, my computer screen showed a gaggle fuck of bouncing junk as the male contestants ran in front of the camera one after the other.

Then the screen changed to a grid format once again, and with a cartoon-like sound effect, boobs popped into their spots on the grid in their oh-so-amazing glory.

Finally! Something worth staring at.

Nipples—large and small—were represented in an excellent variety of skin colors. The women's cup sizes varied as well, but two pairs were obviously man-made. There could be more, it was hard to know for sure without giving them the good squeeze they deserved.

I paused on that screen. Not for a self-indulged hand session, but because I wanted to see if I could recognize Sophia's beautiful breasts. Although I didn't have the photo of her in that wet bikini top (darn Tracy who was so protective of a stranger's privacy in Mexico), the image of her large nipples and areolae was forever etched in my mind.

Are her breasts part of that beautiful line-up?

But no matter how many times I tried to pause the movie, I couldn't get a clear enough shot to know for sure. Two of the women could match what I recalled of her beautiful breasts.

And when the camera panned out to offer an overall view of the set, I spotted an Asian man paired to compete with a muscular red-headed man. Unfortunately, the camera never showed them in any of the up-close shots. Not that it would have allowed me to see Sophia's face hidden in her dark box...

The first game lasted a total of two and a half minutes (at least based on the timer at the bottom of the screen). Two of the men received an erection penalty, one while squeezing one of the marvelous triple-D tits and the other while licking off a very perky but smallish black breast with a large nipple. A vertical line split the screen into two, then a horizontal line split each column into two rows. The commentator narrated a replay of the penalty occurring, zooming in on the men's dicks as they swelled and rose during the game.

I couldn't blame them. My own soldier had become armed and at the ready at some point during the event, but I wanted to resist the urge for now, so I'd only undone the belt of my bathrobe to let myself rise in complete freedom.

12:05 A.M.

THE VIDEO CUT AGAIN with a Batman-like fight-scene flicker, then another dick-matching interlude began with other contestants, one of them dead easy to guess (and immensely ego-killing). With only one black dick in the bunch, it was impossible to get its match wrong. And impossible to feel adequate in comparison to it.

When the grid faded out, the screen showed a row of male contestants again, all butt naked, dicks at rest. Some were short, others tall. Some skinny, some chubby, all with various hairiness levels... Well on their chests and heads at least. All twenty contestants' junk had been shaved to nothing.

The Japanese commentator began talking while drawing new cartoony instructions.

At first, he drew music notes, then an erect dick. Then, a stick figure with an arrow pointing to one of the strange-looking devices being shown in the background. The commentator circled a button on the screen then traded his white pen for a red one. He drew a red circle, then a stick-figure pointing toward the exit.

He traded his pen for a green one, then the word FUCK flashed on the screen followed by the number 25 and some Japanese characters. The symbols + and - appeared, with the same downward arrow and ¥10000 amount I'd seen earlier.

When the penalty disappeared from the screen, the camera panned out to get an overall view of the set. It was as though the porn industry had taken over both the games' projection and sound systems. It was so loud and exciting I had to lower the volume. While I enjoyed my porn and was not ashamed of it, I didn't want to bother those who shared walls with me. Could be a young, jet-lagged family for all I knew.

A loud buzz echoed, not unlike the starting horn at the beginning of a race, and the men hurried into the room and picked their pod as fast as they came in. The closer pods were chosen first.

A few red lights appeared and those contestants left the set.

Those lucky enough to get a green light made the games a lot more interesting to me and my inner voyeur. Each pod had been fitted with a camera, which had the perfect viewing angle. At first it was one green-lit pussy on the screen, then it shrank to display a second, then a third... All shaved and exposed, like a sight for sore eyes. I paused on the screen for a second to better appreciate the view. Lips of all shapes, shades, and sizes. Some thin, some swollen, some large and droopy, some glistening wet, some barely visible. I took a screenshot of that screen so I could use it again later.

While my dick insisted I stare at those beauties a little longer, my brain knew there was a whole lot more to view. I gave myself a couple of pumps then resumed the video, my poor dick only more aroused for it.

The male contestants got busy, obstructing my view on each video thumbnail. A ticking counter appeared below each view, totaling the number of thrusts by each contestant. A few passed the magical number, but none did fewer.

Watching the pussies just after the men left was my favorite part and compelled me to resume my hand job. Too bad they didn't leave that screen on more than a few seconds, but that's why the rewind and pause buttons had been invented.

I particularly liked the one in the bottom left corner: it dripped a small stream. *Maybe a female squirter in the gang?* And the one with the red fingernails in the middle row that showed initiative to finish herself off after the guy left was also pretty inspiring for my taste.

Is this Sophia? She wrote about her red manicure, but did all contestants have red polish on?

I didn't know, but I left the screen paused there for a little while.

After all, I was only a man. And a horny one at that.

Once I'd relieved myself and taken a brief, cold shower, I was back in front of my computer, one hand on my mouse and a cold can of refreshing Sapporo in the other, ready to move on to the next game.

12:30 A.M.

AFTER YET ANOTHER round of the same dick-matching game, the video showed something I hadn't expected: a list of names along with their scores to date.

Will I see Sophia's name?

But as I made my way down through the top ten, I realized the names were not only for the male contestants, but they were also fake: John Thomas, Packer, Mr. P, Schwartz, Schlong, Rod, Peter, Jimmy, Dangler, Johnson, Dick, Willy, Wang, Mr. Winky, etc.

Whoever Mr. Suzuki was, he'd hired someone who spoke English well enough to come up with those clever names. *Does Mr. Suzuki speak English?*

Not that it mattered to me, but John Thomas was currently in the lead.

Once the score disappeared, the Japanese commentator appeared live on the set wearing night-vision goggles and a football helmet. Well... at least his voice sounded like the man who'd been talking while drawing on the screen off camera, but I didn't know for sure (nor did I care).

A camera followed him as he opened the doors leading to another game room that was pitch black. Once fully in the room with the door closed, the camera switched to infrared mode, and the commentator reappeared (kind of). His heat imprint became visible and his silhouette showed him pointing to a corner of the room, where the camera subsequently zoomed in. A woman stood there, but only two sections of her body were visible on thermal, night-vision mode. Whatever material had been used to hide the rest of her was clearly blocking her heat signature. But her breasts and hot pussy were easy to spot with their bright contours.

The camera zoomed out and slowly toured the room. Tits and pussies could be seen above, left, and right. If I died right now, that's what I'd like purgatory to look like: the kind of prison cell my soul could use to expiate my sins of the flesh... Over and over again. Even better if the women hidden in the walls and ceiling were those who'd been my best fucks in this lifetime... I shook that thought away, unsure why it had come to mind in the first place.

The camera then exited the room. Once out and back in regular light, the commentator took off his helmet and goggles, threw them to someone off the frame, then caught a small thing mid-air. The camera zoomed in on his fist: a string dangled from it.

That has to be the tampon Sophia wrote about. Come on, man! Nobody wants to see this...

But I kept looking anyway.

He pulled on the string and released his fist at the same time, showing what the string was attached to. Once again, the camera zoomed in on a very small, see-through tube that contained something cylindrical and white. The tube was smaller than my pinky. He unscrewed it and tapped the tube repeatedly against his palm until a tiny bit of rolled-up parchment paper fell out.

He unrolled it and directed the front toward the camera:

The word BONUS flashed across the screen in the same Batman-like animation.

Then I saw a number written on the minuscule scroll.

A list of bonuses appeared on the screen for a

couple of seconds, then a computer-generated image replaced it. It showed a 3D representation of the room with women's bodies embedded in the walls and ceiling, a bit like what a 3D Battleship board would look like. Naked bodies were aligned either horizontally or vertically on all surfaces. But thankfully for them, none appeared to have their heads below their feet.

The screen split into two, and the left side showed contestants entering the game room with football helmets on. Unlike the commentator, the contestants didn't wear thermal goggles, but such a camera had been fitted in the room. Men were walking blind in that room, hands either reaching toward the ceiling or in front of them. They collided against each other too many times to count. In fact, it was a bit boring to watch. Although I knew Sophia was one of the women hanging from above, this dizzying fumble-in-the-dark game wasn't going to help me see more of her. And soon enough, the thermal lens footage was replaced by regular video footage showing the men exiting the room with their bonuses in hand.

After showing off the number to another camera, the computer-animated mockup of the room started showing colored bodies on the other half of the screen, probably those who'd been claimed already.

A few minutes later, that dull game had come to an end, and so had my beer. I got up and grabbed another one, hopeful that the next game would once again ignite my desires, or at least show me more of Sophia's body.

THE TRANSITIONS HAD BECOME PREDICTABLE. A final set of dicks were matched, and the scores got tabulated once more. Willy had taken the lead, but in my books, I'd gotten at least silver. Out of the variety of ethnicities and physical statures of the contestants, I felt pretty damn proud of my own tool. Okay, not the biggest in the world, but bigger than nineteen out of twenty was a pretty fucking good way to prove what I already knew to be true.

I'm sexy and I know it.

When the camera focused on the set again, the naked men stood with their feet shoulder-width apart, their hands behind their backs, their erect dicks pointing to all angles.

These games are getting worse by the minute.

Where did the ladies go? Bring back those naked pussy cats... Show me the one I'm looking for.

A lineup of Japanese women dressed as school girls appeared out of nowhere and began tossing rings at the male contestants all the while flirting with the camera whenever it approached one of them.

Even though most men moved their hips to try and catch the rings heading their way, let's just admit the school girls' talents didn't involve, include, or have any tie whatsoever with throwing skills. But they *did* look hot in their tiny red and blue outfits.

Damn hot.

Not many rings landed around the men's dicks, and even fewer stayed there. One man with a particularly vertical erection lucked out and got a bonus: a kiss from one of the girls and a ten-thousand-yen prize.

The men walked off the stage, and the Japanese commentator started speaking fast while drawing icons on the screen, which had by now faded to black. First appeared a clock crossed out in red *(not a timed event?)*, then a cartoony ejaculating dick showed a penalty of twenty thousand yen. While the commentator wiped off his scribblings, the camera entered the set where the next game would be held: the room looked like a futuristic, minimalist, and spotless henhouse for giant mechanized chickens.

The video zoomed in on one of the egg-shaped pods for this game and the hand of whoever held the camera pressed a large button.

Ding, ding, ding!

The games once again got interesting.

There it was. In glorious high-def, smack in the middle of my monitor, a splendid, fully shaved, pink pussy. It'd materialized from the bottom up when the button had been pressed. I'd hit that magic button 24/7 if I could. In fact, to the insistence of my dick, I rewound the video a few times. And a few times more.

And then I paused.

If that view could be wrapped up and sold as virtual reality... The world as we know it would end.

And that beautiful image had me abusing myself successfully for the second time since I'd begun watching the games.

I took a screenshot of the World's Best View, and then un-paused the video to see what would be next.

A short pan a second later exposed a little more of the woman's gorgeous ass. Then, a wider pan revealed a small tray next to the egg. On it was a string of five beads—each increasing in size, up to about an inch and a half in diameter—and a conical insert whose widest point was that of the middle bead. Both devices glistened with a thick coat of shiny lube. The camera stayed in this shot, and the commentator began drawing a dick over the pussy, then he drew an arrow pointing from the small tray to her asshole.

He went on way too long with his explanations. The rules had to be more complicated, but who cared? Certainly not me. Instead, I wrapped my hand around my shaft and concentrated on that woman's pussy while he droned on.

Then, through computer-animated ninja trickery that went well beyond my expectations for a private game show that wasn't aimed at the public, the screen showed how a woman was positioned inside the pod. The focus was on a red button in front of her face. A few lightning bolts came out of her ass, and an angry emoticon appeared over her face. Then, the animated woman pushed the button, and the camera zoomed out to show the cartoon man behind her getting crossed off in red.

What?

Then the computer animated video panned out to display a lot of those pods. With tiny popping sounds, women were superimposed to some of the

S.M. PRATT

pods, but not all. The animation continued, with men running into the room and choosing pods. Those who selected an empty pod were crossed off in red as well.

Oh, so being crossed off just means they're out?

Before I could wrap my head around the rules, the black screen transitioned to the male contestants getting ready, putting on condoms, and lining up in a single file.

A few seconds later, the funky porn groove began, and the doors to the game room opened. Men dashed to each select a pod, then they pressed their respective buttons. After half the pods turned bright red one after the other, some contestants left the room. Those lucky enough to have gotten a green pod stayed.

Magically, the screen changed to a tiled version of two rows of five beautiful peaches. My eyes instantly went toward the black beauty and her particularly lippy, swollen pussy at the base of the oval opening. A couple inches higher, her pink anal ring appeared within that same gap in the otherwise solid egg.

Hmmm. I sped up my pace, until a short and skinny man began fucking up my focal point— literally. His small pecker took me right out of my fantasy. I looked at the other available pussies, wondering which was Sophia's.

While I knew my stewardess had selected a pod near the entrance, I didn't know which thumbnail went with each pod. With no carpet of any kind, only skin color could guide my guess. But no matter which was hers, it was definitely a very fine, elegant specimen. The tiny pussy in the top-right corner was getting pounded vigorously, then the first bead of the device got shoved into her ass. The visible part of her green-lit pod turned red and a loud buzz aired over the porn soundtrack.

Too bad. She was pleasant to look at.

But, taking her out made the tiles rearrange themselves to fit into a three-by-three grid, which made them all bigger. Better. My imagination added in their scents, my accelerating fist their warmth, their tightness.

Tiny icons popped on the screen, showing one item for each contestant. More than half had been tagged with a cone. I leaned a bit closer to my screen, focusing on another part of the footage. One woman's folds glistened from her own juices.

But as I got back into a nice rhythm, this time looking at a slick pussy that was being treated like a proper lady with patient, gentle thrusts, a Batman-esque SURPRISE interrupted the video with a vinyl-record scratching sound.

I anxiously waited for them to be done with their long-winded Japanese explanations so I could return to my beautiful images. But when the video feed resumed, the pussies and asses were no longer the focus. Instead, the unlucky contestants who'd been expelled were returning to the set, each walking toward another male contestant.

Team work? Weren't they managing just fine on their own?

The newly returned contestants, confused looks on most of their faces, each picked up the items that the lucky contestants had not elected.

Then another SURPRISE appeared on the screen.

I had absolutely no idea what happened there, but the contestants weren't happy. I even heard one say "No fucking way" in English. That man immediately left the set. Others seemed unsure whether to stay or leave. A loud countdown appeared, seemingly forcing them to decide quickly. The top prize in yen flashed on the screen, along with a large question mark.

What do they have to decide?

But when the countdown reached zero, what happened slowly became clear to me.

The lucky contestants resumed their previous tasks, the unlucky ones took position behind them. The newly-returned unlucky contestants started pushing the device into the previously-lucky-but-definitely-not-lucky-anymore-contestants' asses.

I walked away.

And so did my erection.

Should I turn this off?

While those games now appeared to be on a downward spiral heading way past my comfort zone, they could hold important information... Maybe my stewardess's full name. And maybe I'll see her naked and recognize her. I could actually see her face for the first time.

I returned to sit on the chair at my desk, but covered my eyes with my hands and waited for this game to be over.

But when a cacophony of delighted screams—both male and female—started airing loudly, one after each other, and one on top of each other, I parted my fingers to peek at what was happening.

Not a single man looked offended anymore, save for one guy who was doing the inserting; he was grimacing. The men sandwiched between the pussies and the other men were ALL enjoying the game now. Many sandwiched men were coming right now, their mouths open, their faces almost frozen in awkward ecstasy.

Really?

I took my hands away from my face and noticed that most of them had already retrieved the devices from the women's asses. The final male-male-female threesome was just finishing up, now taking the full screen.

And as they wrapped up that game, the camera showed men fist-pumping each other. The same men who had looked so confused and offended before.

Really? Could it really feel this good?

ALTHOUGH THE LAST bit had been hard to watch, I was heftily rewarded for my patience when the next game started.

The camera zoomed onto an eclectic row of female candidates, all dressed in short skirts and white blouses, hair parted and tied in two ponytails just like my stewardess had described.

Among the group, three brunettes instantly got my attention. I took a screen capture of their faces: the strict-looking one with the luscious lips, the one with shorter hair and the button nose, and the taller one with the Mona Lisa smile.

Which one are you, Sophia?

Can her nails help me identify her?

But the nails of all three brunettes—like those

of many of the contestants—had been painted in one shade of red or another. *Fuck!*

Then, as though the show had been sponsored by an old episode of Baywatch, a horn sounded, and breasts of all sizes started bouncing up and down, left and right in slow motion. A few well-endowed women restrained their movements by pressing them up and against their chest. All three brunettes had either C or D-cups.

Then, one by one, they came to a halt in front of one of the large columns. They all glued their gorgeous red lips onto the surface in front of them. Some columns turned green. As they did, a mini thumbnail of all green feeds began to appear on the screen. Dicks popped out of these openings, and within a few seconds, the lucky contestants' blow jobs were tiled onto my screen, separated into two rows of five videos.

I'd unfortunately lost track of my brunettes in the process. Red lips were hard to differentiate. But how I'd love to re-watch this game once I knew which one she was... Imagining it was my own cock she'd eagerly swallow like that. I'd let her lick it, nibble it, suck it... She could do whatever she wanted to me.

I spat in my palm and resumed stroking my own

shaft, imagining her warm mouth instead of my hand.

Then the video footage showed columns turning to yellow, bringing my attention back to one specific thumbnail. After each turned yellow, the feed switched to another camera, this one within the column itself. One after the other, the male contestants came into a bucket.

Well... In the general direction of that bucket. Some redecorated the walls instead.

UNFORTUNATELY FOR ME, the female game transitions weren't what I'd hoped they'd be.

Mr. Suzuki could have included a pussy and tits matching game, no?

How I would have enjoyed that...

But instead, the camera showed the backstage area where one male contestant was standing in front of a window looking into a mirrored room. A few feet away from him, another man was on his knees. Then, once the camera zoomed out, another male contestant appeared within the shot. He was standing, too, but with his feet slightly below floor level.

A cartoony transition then popped on the screen. It reminded me of those Whack-a-Mole games from carnivals, except that the moles had been replaced with smiling dicks and the mallets with naked women figures bent in half.

The words "Game 6" flashed on the screen and I got to see the set from the female contestants' side of things. It all made sense now. The mirrors were one-sided, like those in police interrogation rooms, except that we weren't looking at murderers, just women lined up in their high heels, super short skirts, and white blouses.

Oh wait!

The blonde's round, naked ass dangled below the hem of her skirt. Then I spotted another one.

They've taken off their panties!

And it's with added vigor that I resumed priming my pump.

I forgave Mr. Suzuki for not including the transition I'd have loved to see the second I realized he'd placed cameras under the floor instead.

The sight was priceless. A lineup of pussies between sets of high heels. Some shier than others, some boldly exposed between parted legs. All of it to the same groovy porn beat.

I bet they didn't even know there were cameras under the floor!

So worth it!

A gong sounded, and I focused on the button-nosed brunette as she ran toward a black circle against the back wall. A loud countdown appeared on the screen. When it reached zero, the gong sounded again and the cameras switched to various new angles. I'd lost track of my brunette, but I'd gained the ideal view on all my lovely pussies.

Some got poked at. Some stayed put for a few seconds, without any action. Some left and went to a different spot, including one that left a streak of her moisture on the mirrored surface as she slid down before leaving.

Hmmm.

With one hand handling my weapon and the other fiddling with the rewind, play, and pause buttons on my keyboard, I'd say my needs were being met.

I had the best seat in the house, short of owning one of those lucky dicks that got to feel the warmth and tightness of those gorgeous pussies.

The one in the top corner tile had generous folds that parted easily when the dick behind the wall pushed through its opening. Her red fingernails made an appearance, ever so briefly, as she grabbed her ass just behind her pussy and parted herself a little. She slid down and slammed her ass flat on the mirrored wall. Then again, and again.

Come on, baby. Keep it up.

Small numbers popped on top of each of the tiles, all numbers increasing steadily, along with my excitement.

As I enjoyed matching her rhythm, another pussy took over the main shot. The large-lippy specimen was being pushed by a monster of a black dick behind her. Another camera captured her jaw as it dropped, then her eyes nearly popped out of their sockets as she reached behind her and wrapped her hands around that humongous appendage.

A Batman-esque interruption appeared again, this time Japanese characters followed by a question mark.

She spat on her hands, then spread her spit onto the tip of the cock poking at her, making it glisten. She aligned herself with the man behind the wall, her head looking between her legs. Then she faced forward as she pushed backward onto the man, barely hiding the tip of the man's tool in her pussy. The screen was now split in two. One camera focused on her heaving bosoms as she inhaled and exhaled deeply; the other on her pussy and the major deconstruction work about to happen there.

How is this even going to fit?

Then, she lowered herself more: a good two inches of him disappeared into her body. A loud cry came out of her. Then, she slowly pulled herself away, her eyes turned backwards, as though she'd passed out.

A loud alarm sounded, and the screen zoomed away from the woman in deep pain (or pleasure?) and focused on another female competitor. She was heading toward the finish line, her tits joyfully bouncing along until she reached the announcer and high-fived him.

AFTER SHOWING AN UPDATED score board with fake names, the screen flashed with the words "Game 7".

The camera showed a new set—yet again—with just ten men sitting with a beer in hand, smiling at the camera. Their upper bodies were leaning back against blue beach chairs, but I had no idea what they were sitting on since their lower bodies were hidden underneath a large horizontal surface with an old-fashioned joystick on it.

As though they had read my mind, the screen shifted to a computer animation showing their sitting arrangement. It showed a man, butt naked (big surprise), with his flaccid equipment dangling between his legs through a hole in the chair. The hole wasn't big enough for the man's ass to go through, but large enough for his junk and some of his butt crack to benefit from the breeze below (or whatever the purpose of that hole was).

Night-vision cameras then showed the assortment of sacks and dicks dangling in their own thumbnails. It wasn't cold in there based on how low things dangled.

The Japanese commentator began speaking faster while drawing his rule icons.

It showed various times along with bonuses. For each additional 15 seconds, the male contestants would receive a bonus of 10,000 yen, up to 100,000 yen. Then the commentator moved the joystick, which showed a matching camera with night-vision settings. The word BONUS flashed on the screen. The commentator drew tits and wrote 10,000 yen. He then drew a pussy with the same bonus amount.

A countdown began ticking down on the screen. When it reached 0, nothing happened, except for men raising their beer bottles and cheering each other from a distance.

Beer drinking can't be what they're being timed on?

But the next footage clarified things. A horizontal line split the screen into two. The top part still showed the men resting on their chairs. Some drinking, some moving the joystick, but most doing both. The bottom section of the screen was dark green, in night-vision mode with women crawling on all fours, their bodies hot, especially their pussies, but they disappeared out of sight after turning out of the camera's angle.

Then the screen split into ten thumbnails which likely displayed what the men were controlling with their joysticks because most of the shots made me dizzy. Then some of the images started making sense. A woman, still crawling on all fours, but this time facing the camera. Her hair appeared wet, her eyes weirdly freakish-looking in that mode, but thankfully the man zoomed onto something else. The woman straightened her back and sat up. She collected her ponytails and brought them behind her back, pushing her tits forward in the process. Even in night-vision mode, her areolae were noticeable, her nipples showing concentrated heat. A loud "cha-ching" sound played and this man's thumbnail showed a 10,000 bonus.

When the first fifteen seconds had elapsed, all thumbnails showed another 10,000 bonus.

I glanced at the other thumbnails, most of them now much steadier. One showed a woman still walking toward the camera, the man zoomed onto the long crevice between her dangling breasts as they swayed in her shirt. A bonus was added to his thumbnail.

On the next one, an agile tongue tickled a sack, then the woman's mouth opened wide and she fit the entire thing in her mouth. *Like what Sophia described in her journal. Is this her mouth?*

My own equipment responded, wishing it had been the chosen sack. I wrapped my hand around it while my other hand pumped away to a great shot of a woman's pussy seen from behind. She was on all fours, her knees nearly shoulder-width apart, her skirt only covering the top of her ass; her entire crack and pussy gleamed. A line of sweat (or juices) was running down her inner thighs. That man deserved the bonus that appeared on his video stream. I also deserved a souvenir of that, so I took a screenshot.

I swear the heat of the event somehow transcended time and place and had me sweating at this very second. There was so much visual stimulation coming at me, I couldn't focus on trying to spot Sophia based on her journal entries.

Some thumbnails disappeared, making more room for the remaining ones. Another great shot grabbed my attention. This one was a close-up shot of someone's wet pussy. Her female juices had collected to form a drip which was ready to fall off any second now. *Cha-ching!*

Then a tongue licked the invisible line from a man's balls to his asshole. She pushed apart the man's cheeks and pushed the tip of her tongue into his hole. The camera was zoomed enough to show the man's dick engorge as she kept tickling his back end. A red line was drawn across the feed, and his thumbnail disappeared.

More and more thumbnails disappeared one after the other soon thereafter, and I decided to finish myself off. I rewound to that glorious ass and pussy shot and gave it my all, imagining that it was my mystery stewardess I was staring at (because it could very well have been).

PLEASED WITH MYSELF, I cracked open another cold beer before resuming the rest of the games. The progress bar showed very little time remaining, so I assumed only one game was left. Sophia had described a fantastic game, and I was pretty sure it was coming up next.

When I resumed the video, it was everything I hoped it'd be... and more. So many beautiful women receiving pleasure without men being visible and ruining my fantasy.

While I knew the male contestants were fucking them from below, I imagined I was the one doing it to them. The blonde woman was arching her back so much she had to be a gymnast. I swear her head almost touched the floor. She had long let go of her remote and had decided to rip her shirt apart instead. She was fumbling with her augmented tits as her body pulsed from the pounding she was receiving from underneath the set.

Then I remembered my goal and looked at the three brunettes instead.

Which is Sophia?

The button-nosed brunette with the shorter hair was getting fucked in the pussy, not the ass. She was riding that cock like a good cowgirl, using her knees to lift and lower herself onto the man below. *Not her!*

The one with the luscious lips didn't look strict at all anymore. She looked high on her own orgasmic tsunami. *Is this Sophia?* Her entire body rocked with whatever the man below was doing to her. She was glued to her seat, so I couldn't even tell which orifices were occupied.

I found the last brunette and focused on her. Her eyes were closed, her Mona Lisa smile replaced by a slanted smirk that widened as her brow furrowed. Her mouth opened, her groans became audible over the porn soundtrack and then her eyes opened and spoke volume as to the intensity of her orgasm. She reached up for the remote and pulled on it, splashing her arched back with a mixture of water and melting ice pellets. Her now transparent shirt showcased the erect nipples I'd fantasized about for months.

Sophia...

I didn't need to see the purple vibrator being retrieved below her pussy to know she was the one. I could have recognized those beautiful breasts anywhere.

I rewound that last game and re-watched the entire thing, only paying attention to my no-longer mysterious Sophia.

She. Was. Hot.

Everything about her was perfect. She was obviously lost in her own universe while getting fucked. She moved so sensually, so instinctually. Her face and body were beautiful, but I wasn't sure if I liked her mind and thoughts more... At least the ones she put down in her diary.

She's quite something, this Sophia.

How I would have liked to be the one taking care of her right then and there.

I took a screenshot of her when she looked straight at the camera. Her traits were beautiful in a regular, pretty girl-next-door kind of way... until she smiled... or came.

When I reached the end of the video, applauses filled the air when the last woman finally came.

Then the screen went dark. No credits. Nothing.

Too bad. I'd have liked to see the contestants' names, but it was still the best 100,000 yen I'd ever spent.

My hard-on was roaring, but I restrained myself and didn't watch the entire thing right away. I could do it later.

And again and again later.

But right now, I had a promise to fulfill.

2:03 A.M.

I PICKED up the phone and dialed Keiki's room number.

"Hey, it's me. I finished my video."

"Great, I'll be right there."

Not even thirty seconds went by before I heard a discreet knock on my door.

I walked over, tying up my robe and doing my best to hide my erection by tucking my shaft under my belt.

Upon opening the door, she whispered to me while she slid something in my bathrobe's pocket: "Stick to the plan. When you get upset later, read that note."

Then, she walked in, leaving my mind puzzled and my cock deflated.

What the fuck?

My hand dove in my robe pocket which now contained a thick pile of folded papers.

She'd already sat on my bed and was speaking up when I turned around. "So, how were your games? Worth it?" she asked, looking at my laptop, whose monitor had turned to screen-saving mode.

"Fuck yeah!" I said, confused but playing along. "Drink?" I offered.

"Sure, I'll take another whiskey if you still have some."

I opened the fridge to see. I poured her a drink in the glass she'd left behind earlier and grabbed another beer for myself.

I walked it over to her.

She took a sip, then smiled at me with devious intent. Although I wasn't sure, I could have sworn she whispered the word "Now" at that point.

I looked at her for confirmation, and she gave me a slight nod.

Game on, then!

I drank a large sip of my beer, then placed my can on the corner of the desk before taking her drink away from her mid-sip. I pushed her shoulders back and she landed flat onto my bed, so I straddled her.

"What are you doing?" she asked.

"Taking what I want," I said. "I'm doing what I've been thinking about ever since I met you," I said unzipping her jeans and trying to pull the fabric down her legs.

Damn these things are tight. I managed to lower them enough to reach mid-thighs. *Fuck'em. They can stay there. Plenty of room for me.*

"No!" she said, reaching for the waist of her jeans and starting to undo my hard work.

But I took care of that by pulling her top off over her head. Her arms simply had to follow or they'd break.

Her turtleneck out of the way, I admired her bright yellow bra for a second and noticed it clipped in the front.

"Stop what you're doing!" she said, this time a little louder.

She had me fucking confused now. But I swear she once again nodded at me, ever so slightly. With one hand, I undid her bra and exposed her tits.

"Gorgeous breasts, like you said." My lips went for one of her small nipples while my hands pulled the straps past her arms.

"Stop!" she yelped.

"The neighbors will hear you. You gotta shut up!" I ordered.

"No, I won't keep quiet unless you make me," she said.

I untied the belt of my thick terry-cloth bathrobe and pulled it out of its loops. "That'll do. I'll have my way with you," I threatened before placing the belt in her mouth and tying it behind the back of her head.

Her eyes didn't shine with fear, just with fun.

Fuck, this is confusing.

I flipped her small body so her stomach and beautiful tits were now resting on the comforter. Doing so exposed a tattoo that began on her lower back and finished underneath her panties: cherry blossoms in shades of black, red, and pink.

Didn't expect that at all!

But seeing her in this position gave me an idea. I reached for the ends of the belt that hung behind her head and I tied her wrists behind her back.

Now free to do as I pleased in near silence (after all, she was putting on a good show with the muffled mumbling), I pulled her jeans farther down. This time, I took my sweet time, and I got them fully off, one leg at a time.

Now naked save for her yellow panties and that terry-cloth belt, I parted her legs. My fingers grazed the fabric of her underwear. Her excitement had already left a wide, dark, wet spot that I caressed.

Damn. She's really into this shit. First I only scraped over the fabric, then I let the tip of one of my fingers glide underneath it.

Her legs closed on me when I did that, but I brought her hips to the edge of the bed and sat myself with my face right between her legs. Her scent was invigorating, inviting, and too potent to ignore.

I moved the wet fabric over to the side. She moaned through the belt, and the moans got louder when the tip of my tongue tickled the hairiest pussy I'd licked in a long time. But her musky, salty taste made it worth it.

I hated to destroy beautiful underwear, but I followed her instructions and ripped her panties right off her, revealing the rest of her gorgeous tattoo. I brought her lower body up on the bed again, my open bathrobe letting my cock free to stand gloriously over her gorgeous tattoo background.

I ditched my robe and let it fall on the floor, then walked over to my suitcase for my stash of condoms.

When I returned to the bed, Keiki had rolled herself up in a ball and was now facing the bedroom door.

Her own words echoed in my mind as I made

my way around the bed to look at her. *"I may even cry, but I'll be loving every moment of it."*

Tears were indeed streaming down her face.

What the fuck? With three fingers, I tilted her chin and made eye contact with her. She winked at me.

I pulled the belt out of her mouth, to see if she would say the safety word, but no. Nothing but quiet cries came out of her lips.

This was new territory to me, but heck, she winked at me again and I knew I had to go on.

I sat her up on the bed, her hands were still tied behind her back.

"If you don't like the belt in your mouth, maybe you'd like to try this instead," I said, attempting to shove the tip of my cock in her mouth, but she shut her lips tightly.

"Then if not there, I'll have to find somewhere else for me to fuck you." I pushed her on her back again, then spread open her legs. Cat-like cries started coming out of her mouth. I shoved my index finger into her pussy. It slid in like a hot knife in butter. I added another digit. "Should I fuck you in your hairy pussy, or would you prefer it in the ass?"

Her only reply was a shake of the head.

I pulled out my fingers and used her own

moisture to lube her ass. Then I pushed my pinky in.

Her cat-like noises went up in pitch and she started panting.

"Is this what you want then?"

My pinky kept tickling her ass as my mouth ripped open the condom I held with my non-dominant hand. Good thing I'd had years of practice unrolling condoms with either of my hands. A second later, I was armed and ready. I parted her legs even more, then pushed the tip of my cock into her wet pussy. My right pinky was busy maintaining its post, but I used my left hand to turn her face toward me.

I needed to see her expression. I needed to reassure myself I was doing the right thing.

Her eyes were now red from crying, her mouth barely open, the kitty-like cries nearly silent. I brought myself up and close to her face.

"Keiki?" I whispered.

"Go," she whispered back.

"No?" I repeated louder.

She shook her head. *Fuck. What does that mean?*

"Do you want me to fuck you like a Samurai?" I asked her, hoping that my question would remind her of the safety word and she'd use it.

"No!" she said.

I rammed into her while our eyes were locked on each other's. She smiled for a split second, then resumed her kitty-like groans and cries.

This is messed-up shit.

But I'd already wasted enough time second-guessing myself. It was too fucking late for that. She was too fucking wet, and I'd given her plenty of chances to really stop me.

I rammed and rammed into her, hitting the back of her small womb as I thrust deeply into her pussy. I closed my eyes and imagined she was Sophia. Now that I could picture her face, her tits, her pussy... It wasn't long until I burst in excitement, and from the pussy contracting around my shaft as I started catching my breath again, I knew Keiki had had a good time as well.

2:25 A.M.

I GRABBED my robe from the floor, put it on, untied Keiki so I could get my belt back, and then walked into the bathroom.

After cleaning myself up and splashing a bit of water on my face—coming to terms with a new threshold I'd never thought I'd pass—I went back into the room. Keiki was getting dressed. She had a big smile on her face.

"That's really what you wanted?" I asked.

"It was perfect. Thanks!" she said.

I let that wave of relief wash over me. I opened the fridge and grabbed a cold bottle of water. I lifted it up and looked at her. "Sure," she said.

I tossed it her way, then grabbed one for me as well. "Nice tattoo, by the way. Are you part of a gang?" I asked jokingly before sitting myself next to her on the bed.

"Funny you mention that..."

"What do you mean?"

"I'm not, but these men we got the video from, they're with the Japanese mafia. They've been recording you since you got back, including our little fun here, and they will have no issue releasing this video to our employer if you don't return the USB stick you got from them."

"What?"

I stared her down, giving her a chance to say she was joking. *She has to be.* But she didn't budge.

"Why would I? I paid for it fair and square."

She shook her head. "No, you only paid for the opportunity to watch it."

"What? Says who? I want to keep it."

"If you keep it, then they'll upload the video of you fucking me against my will on the internet. They can hack their way to any site, including our airline's. Wouldn't that look lovely on the home page? I'm sure it would make a big difference to your career. And mine."

Fuck. I replayed what else I'd done in my room while watching the games. *I don't want that footage out either...*

"No, you're not going to want to release that video. You're in it as well."

"Charlie, it's not *me*. It's *them*. My involvement was dictated by that man in the restaurant. He's waiting for me in the lobby. I need to return the stick and the camera very shortly. They said that if I don't cooperate with them, and if you don't give back the stick, they'll force me to report you to the police as a rapist."

"Now, that's FUCKING GREAT," I yelled, getting up.

"Hey, lower your voice and don't be mad at me. That's what I was referring to earlier," she said, her eyes going from the pocket of my robe to my eyes.

But a thick pile of papers wasn't going to help me calm down.

"How the fuck did they get a camera in here?" I inspected the room. "Where is it?"

Keiki tilted her head toward the wall near the door.

I couldn't see anything. Then I saw it. A tiny screw-like object just below a picture frame. In the middle of it, a tiny pin-sized hole with a lens. "You fucking put it there?" I asked, ripping the thing off the wall.

It wasn't attached to anything.

"How does it work? It's not connected to any wires."

Keiki was looking down, shaking her head. "The man said to just place it where it would have a good view of the bed and he ordered me to stage that little scene with you. That part of the plan was kind of fun, though. You have to admit..."

I shook my head at her.

"Did you think this through? What's to prevent them from releasing the video anyway? What's to prevent them from blackmailing us for the rest of our lives?"

"Well... I don't know. I just want this all to disappear. They've got bigger fish to fry than embarrassing us both or destroying our lives, no?"

I paced the room, inhaling and exhaling deeply.

How can the best day of my life also be the worst?

"They say bright ideas often come in the shower. Want to give it a try?" she asked, her eyes once again going from my robe pocket to my eyes.

I grabbed my cellphone and then locked myself in the bathroom. Maybe she'd written more information in those papers. And if not, maybe Google would have a fucking solution to getting out of a Japanese Mafia blackmail situation.

3:30 A.M.

AFTER READING and re-reading her pages, I'd
gotten the gist, but I wasn't any closer to a solution.
She spent two paragraphs apologizing profusely
before listing the facts she knew based on what the
man had said:

   - The camera captures audio and video with
180-degree coverage.

   - The laptop must be close to the camera to
receive the signal, so chances are it doesn't
broadcast anything live. It probably records it onto
the stick.

   - Attempting to copy the game video to a hard
drive will wipe your computer clean.

   - If the man in the lobby doesn't receive the
stick back by 4 a.m., he'll come and get it himself or

track us down anywhere in the world. There's a tracking device on the stick.

- The man will check to see if I recorded the video he needed.

And the list went on about threats he'd made to Keiki and her family. It fully explained why she'd been so shaky on the walk back to the hotel.

So, I can't destroy the camera. I can't destroy the stick. I can't copy the video.

That means I can't fucking prevent them from blackmailing me and Keiki for the rest of our lives.

Can I go to the police with that? Or is it possible for the Japanese Mafia to be in cahoots with the local authorities?

Fuck. Fuck. Fuck.

And I don't understand enough about computers to get myself out of this shit.

...But I know a guy who does!

I unlocked my phone and found the contact information for the hacker who'd been so helpful to me a few weeks prior.

I couldn't really call him because I didn't know how sensitive that camera microphone was. I texted him. It was early here, but thankfully the time difference worked in my favor. He should be up.

Hey bud.
I'm in trouble.

Can you help me right now?

A couple of minutes elapsed, then I saw the three dots indicating he was typing a reply.

What's going on?

I described the situation as succinctly as I could and then waited.

Send me photos of camera and list of files on stick.

Give me a minute.

I walked into the room. Keiki was looking at me, hope in her eyes.

"Hey, would you do me a great favor?" I asked her.

She pursed her lips. "Sure, what?"

"Since I can't keep that video, I'd like to at least have a souvenir of this evening. Would you mind posing for me?"

She had a crooked smile on her face. "Okay..."

But when I instructed her to take her top off and sit right next to the camera, the light bulb lit up in her eyes.

I took two photos. One for me, with Keiki in her

bra. The other for my hacker, with Keiki out of the zoomed in area.

"And how about you take that gorgeous bra off and sit right here," I said, tapping next to my laptop. "And we could take a few more?"

"Sure," she said.

The camera lens was now facing down against the desk, so it shouldn't see what I was taking pictures of, but it probably still recorded the sound.

I put in my password to get rid of the screensaver and then clicked my way to the window that showed the list of files on the USB stick. Then I took two pictures as well, their focus—and purpose—very different from one another.

"Thanks, Keiki. These photos may come handy for future solo sessions," I said before walking back into the bathroom.

I sent the two images my hacker needed and waited patiently.

Don't touch these files.
You want me to wipe the stick clean?

No, they'll check to ensure the videos are there.
Can you delete the new video file only, but not right now?
On a timer or something?

How much time do I have to code this?

I looked at the clock on my phone before typing my reply.

20 minutes before I have to return the stick.
Could you activate that timer in 24 hours?

OK.
I'll email you a file in 15.
Leave that stick connected when you open my email.
Double-click the attachment.
I'll take care of the rest.

I GOT DRESSED while waiting for that precious email.

Right on time, my man delivered.

After following the instructions I received, I ejected the USB drive from my computer and gave back my most prized possession to Keiki.

"Do you want me to take it to the man downstairs?" I asked.

"I have to do it. But could you come with me, if you don't mind?"

"Of course, I'll go with you."

She placed the camera and the stick in the same black plastic bag, and then we left my room.

The elevator ride down was spent in total silence. I let Keiki walk ahead of me in the lobby.

As promised, the scrawny man was patiently sitting alone, reading a newspaper. When he saw us, he got up.

Keiki handed him the same bag he'd given her hours earlier. He pointed to the empty seats in front of him and we sat down.

He pulled up a small laptop from a little pouch that had been resting next to him. He powered it up, inserted the stick, and then double-clicked on one of the files. After turning the screen so all of us would see what he was doing, a small video window popped up, showing me at the computer. He fast-forwarded until it showed the both of us on the bed. Under other circumstances, I'd have probably enjoyed watching my own performance. But not right now. Not like this.

The man then clicked on the other video file, the one I'd watched earlier. For a brief few seconds, he fast-forwarded through some of the moments I'd enjoyed hours before.

Then it was over.

He ejected the stick, closed the small laptop, packed it away along with the stick and camera, then nodded at Keiki before saying something in Japanese and leaving the hotel lobby.

A minute must have elapsed before either of us moved or said anything.

"What did he say?" I asked.

"Pleasure doing business with you."

I exhaled and prayed that the hidden file my hacker had added to the stick would work its magic as promised.

We rode the elevator up again.

"I'm fucking glad this is behind us now," I said.

"What's the solution you came up with?" she finally asked.

"When we board our flight, the latest video on that stick will self-destruct. Or, if anyone attempts to copy it elsewhere, it will also self-destruct."

"And how did you do that?"

"I know a guy."

NEXT STEPS

THAT JAPANESE LAYOVER was officially the craziest shit I'd ever gotten myself into.

But Keiki's words when we parted ways a few hours later made me feel better.

I quote: "And your reputation is well deserved. Glad to have had my test run, even though it was under strange circumstances."

I don't believe my mystery stewardess knew who was behind those games, but I'm sure glad I finally have a face that I can see when I think of her now.

And those screenshots I took?

Priceless. They've added countless details to my wet dreams.

I've got one last entry to revisit in her journal.

And now that I know what she looks like, I could think of a way to track her down for real... finally.

Her Spanish layover—more like an extended vacation—was much closer to regular life than her Japanese experience, and she did make a few one-on-one connections with Spaniards that she may have wanted to maintain, so it's not too far-fetched to believe that she may still be in contact with them today.

I'm looking forward to snacking on delicious *tapas* and inexpensive Rioja wines while tracking her down.

TO BE CONTINUED...

...IN PART 10 of *The Stewardess's Diary*, available at most major book retailers.

The complete episodic novel is also available in one (thick) paperback with exclusive author's notes about the series and what inspired each episode.

ABOUT THE AUTHOR

S.M. Pratt is a single woman traveling the world on her own, living in the moment, looking for more than love, and always trying out new things. Fun adventures and unique cultural experiences are always at the top of her agenda, no matter the country she happens to be visiting.

She would love to quit her day job and write full-time. You can help her write the next story faster by purchasing her books and/or giving her five-star reviews. Without your support, she's invisible and unable to make a living doing what she loves, which is creating what you love to read.

If you haven't done so already, please join her private reader group for previews, exclusive offers, and more. It's free: https://smpratt.com

For more information:
smpratt.com
info@smpratt.com